Keeper
of the
Atlas

Book 1 of The Atlas Chronicles ®

Karolyn Timarkos

Little White Dog
Publishing

www.theatlaschronicles.com

The Atlas Chronicles ® is owned by Karolyn Timarkos 2012

Text © Karolyn Timarkos 2002, 2015, 2016
Cover Design © Karolyn Timarkos 2016
Runes © Karolyn Timarkos 2015

First published by Little White Dog Publishing 2014
This edition published 2016

ISBN 978-0-473-34042-1

A CIP Catalogue record for this book is available from the National Library of New Zealand Te Puna Matauranga o Aotearoa.

The right of Karolyn Timarkos to be identified as the author of this work and illustrator of the runes has been asserted by her. www.karolyntimarkos.com

For my wonderful Mum, Shirley Porter.
For everything.

Contents

1: A Mysterious Apparition

Briana Ryan stared at the strange-looking creature who had appeared between the trunks of two kowhai trees in a puff of green smoke. Her first impression was of a little old man, until her brain quickly registered two facts. One: he was only the height of a toddler. Two: he couldn't possibly be human.

She had been running back toward their house from the neighbour's, cursing her twin brother Hamish in time to her strides, when the creature appeared. Hamish hadn't come home at the appointed time from his sleep-over at Lachlan's house, or answered his phone, so Briana had been sent to fetch him.

Hamish was no longer in sight. Briana was the fastest girl in her year at school, but she couldn't keep up with her brother, who had run around the corner of the chickens' shed before the creature appeared.

The storm that had died out in the early hours of the morning had reasserted itself with a deluge as the twins left

Lachlan's. Briana wiped her long black hair off her face, stared at the creature, and jumped when he spoke to her in a thick Welsh accent similar to her Uncle Wynn's. "My Lady, you have to take Rashid with you."

She approached him cautiously. "What?"

"Hamish took Rashid out of your suitcase and locked him in his wardrobe. You have to take Rashid with you to Wales." He glanced toward the shed. "You have to take him." Clasping a gold necklace with a rectangular icon hanging from it, he said what sounded like 'Ripple out', and disappeared in another puff of green smoke.

Briana was still staring at the spot where the creature had disappeared when Hamish came back around the corner of the shed.

"Briana, what the hell are you doing? The olds are going to kill us, get a move on."

"Us? You're the one in trouble, not me," she snapped back, before gathering herself together and running along behind Hamish again, her thoughts in turmoil about what had happened.

There wouldn't be any point mentioning the creature to Hamish. Briana often rolled her eyes at his obsession with all that stupid sci-fi and fantasy stuff, so he would presume she was winding him up. As for telling Mum and Dad, well, not after the scandal at school last week with those silly Year 11 girls. If Briana told her parents a strange non-human creature had spoken to her after appearing in a puff of green smoke, they would think she was also taking drugs.

Then the answer hit her, and confusion turned to a grudging appreciation of Christopher's talent. Lachlan's older brother, who lived in Auckland, was in his final year of a Diploma in Applied Animation at Unitec.

The creature had looked real, and Briana hadn't seen the projection unit, or even the speakers or microphone. They must have been camouflaged to blend in with the grass and trees or something.

It was an awful day to choose to be outside projecting animations though. And there was no way Christopher could have predicted Briana would run past that particular point at that particular time. The only reason she had been there was Hamish and Lachlan hadn't answered their cell phones or the landline, so Briana had run next door to get her brother. Unless, oh, of course, this was some kind of stupid practical joke Hamish had organised with Christopher and Lachlan. That's why they hadn't answered their phones. Typical. Well, she wouldn't give them the satisfaction. She wouldn't mention the creature to Hamish at all.

When she arrived back at their house, she could hear Mum yelling at Hamish. "Why didn't you ... ? Couldn't you . . . ?" Mum took a deep breath before continuing, and managed to finish a sentence. "How dare you be late? I told you to make sure Briana didn't have to come and get you, and look at the state of you both. Hamish, I have a good mind to . . ." She stopped with a gasp, raising her hands to her temples.

Dad put a supporting arm around Mum. "Now see what you've done, you've given Isabel one of her headaches again. Get inside and change your clothes right now. You have four minutes or we'll leave you behind." Hamish bolted in the house.

Over the past few weeks the twin's mother had been

getting bad headaches, and seemed drained of energy. Her regular doctor had been away, and the one she saw instead said it was some sort of bug or virus. He gave her headache and nausea tablets. Briana thought a second (and probably better) opinion from Doctor Trish would be a good idea, but when the headaches had stopped Mum hadn't bothered to make an appointment. Now, it seemed, they were back again.

Dad turned to Briana, struggling to get his temper under control. "Thanks Bree." Looking at her soaking clothes he added, "You'd better get changed too. Sorry."

Briana went inside to the hall closet, where she grabbed a towel and dried her hair as best she could. So much for the half hour she'd spent styling it earlier. With her hair in a towel turban, she headed for Hamish's room. Dad's creepy cousin David, a retired farmer, and his awful daughter, Cheryl, were going to look after the farm while the Ryans went to Wales for a holiday. Cheryl would be staying in Briana's room, despite all of Briana's protests. She had moved everything she owned into Hamish's enormous wardrobe, which her brother had bolted and padlocked.

He had told Briana, "If we don't take precautions we'll come home and find everything we own sold on TradeMe."

David and Cheryl were also the reason the twins had taken their four cats, Briana's males Einstein and Schrödinger, and Hamish's females Romana and Karina, to Lachlan's house last night so people they trusted could look after them. Briana had a tear-filled goodbye with her two, and had cried herself to sleep last night at the thought of leaving them for so long.

When she entered Hamish's bedroom, he was changed already, having swapped his wet Shark Alley board shorts and

T-shirt for dry Shark Alley board shorts and T-shirt. He had secured sponsorship last year from the surf wear company after winning several events in the Surfing New Zealand Grom Series for surfers under the age of sixteen, and he wore Shark Alley clothing proudly and consistently, unless he had a sci-fi T-shirt on. Grinning at Briana as he walked out of the room he tossed her the key.

"Don't forget to lock it".

Briana went to the wardrobe in a panic, as her best clothes were packed. Squeezing into a pair of jeans she had really grown out of, she matched them with the most stylish top she had of those she was leaving behind. Remembering the animated creature's warning, she looked up, and sure enough, there was her toy monkey, Rashid, stuffed on a top shelf.

It was weird Christopher would use the animation to tell her about Rashid, but there was no time to worry about that for now. After pulling Rashid down she closed the doors, and freaked out as she saw herself in the mirror on the door. Her make-up had run everywhere in the rain. Dashing into the bathroom, she threw her wet clothes on the floor, and had just cleaned her ruined make-up off when Dad came in looking for her. "Bree, sorry honey, but we really have to go now."

"I have to put my make-up back on."

"Sweetie, there's no time. We're behind schedule already, and in this terrible weather it will be a slow drive to Auckland. Thank goodness it's a Sunday so the traffic won't be as bad as during the week."

Briana looked at her watch. "Dad, it's only 9.40, so 10.40, 11.40, we'll be at the airport by 12.40 at the latest, and the flight's not until 2.30 this afternoon."

"We have to check in three hours beforehand."

"Seriously? Dad, you're so old fashioned. It's only ninety minutes these days, and besides, they can't check everyone in at the same time."

Dad gave her *that* look.

"Fine, I'll do it in the car. I'll need to get my make-up bag out of my suitcase."

"Bree, it is bucketing out there, and your suitcase is behind all of ours. You'll have to wait until we get to Auckland."

"But . . ."

"No."

"Can't I . . ."

"No." Dad said sharply, then apologised. "I'm sorry, I'm angry at Hamish not you, but we have to go."

She looked at him for a moment, before exclaiming, "I hate Hamish." Picking up her wet clothes, she stopped to stuff them into a plastic bag in the kitchen, and then ran to the van with the bag in one hand, and Rashid in the other.

Mum looked over her shoulder. "Oh Briana, you're not seriously going to wear those jeans? Honey, they're too small for you."

Hamish smirked at his sister. "Mum, if Bree wants to suffer in the name of fashion, it's her right to make that choice, and we should respect it." He let out a mock cry of repulsion. "Oh my gosh darn, it walks in daylight without make-up on, arrgghh, the horror."

Dad looked in the rear vision mirror. "You're in a lot of trouble right now, young man. Stop teasing your sister and apologise to her this instant."

"Sorry Briana." The smirk, and the use of her full name, conveyed his true sentiments, but Briana let it slide. She understood her brother well enough to know if she stopped biting, he'd stop teasing.

Hamish looked at Rashid. "Oh, you found him, did you?" He continued softly so Mum and Dad wouldn't hear. "You know you're really weird, right? You're obsessed with fashion and looking perfect, you wouldn't be seen dead in public without make-up, but you insist on bringing that old thing on holiday with us. You're a little too old to be so attached to a cuddly-wuddly monkey-wonkey."

Briana, refusing to take the bait, turned away from him and looked out the window, hugging Rashid close.

She couldn't explain herself why she was still so attached to the toy monkey she had been given when she was born. All her friends had grown out of sentimental attachments to stuffed toys and considered them uncool. Briana would be mortified if any of them found out she still slept with one. Her brother occasionally used this knowledge for black-mailing her into doing his homework for him. And it wasn't only Rashid. Briana had a whole menagerie of stuffed toys that meant the world to her (all currently locked in Hamish's wardrobe).

Every so often she would be somewhere, a zoo, museum, or toyshop, would see a certain soft toy, and simply have to buy it. It was some sort of compulsion she was powerless to resist.

As Dad drove toward Auckland, Briana tried to maintain her rancour with Hamish, but she was too excited to remain angry for long. Before today, she had never been further away from Tauranga than Wellington. Now they were going to the other side of the world to spend time with Mum's younger sister, Alys, and her husband, Wynn.

Aunty Alys and Uncle Wynn lived in Abergavenny, a small town in southeast Wales where Briana's great-great-grand-father was born, before moving to New Zealand with his parents at a young age. It was cool that Briana would soon celebrate her sixteenth birthday in the country where she could trace her ancestry back a thousand years.

Dad had a business acquaintance who owned a motel close to Auckland International Airport, and had offered to mind the Ryan's van while they were away. After dropping the vehicle off, the family caught the motel's shuttle bus to the terminal, and Briana carefully reapplied her make-up as they drove toward the airport, her excitement building.

Over twenty-four hours later, Briana was less excited; shattered and exhausted by the two long haul flights, and the fact she had been unable to sleep the entire time while sitting upright. Hamish had watched movies all the way to Los Angeles, and then slept eight hours straight after leaving LAX.

After arriving in London, Briana reset her watch to the correct time and day (4:50 a.m. on Monday). The family collected their luggage, cleared customs, and then Dad went off to collect the rental car while Mum and the twins grabbed a light breakfast, despite Hamish's protest that their body clocks demanded dinner.

It was 7.00 a.m. when they left the terminal, and an icy blast assaulted them as they stepped outside. Briana quickly opened her suitcase and dug out her thick, fleece-lined purple and pink ski-jacket, a hat, and a pair of gloves. Hamish, who surfed all through winter at home, pranced around in his T-shirt and board shorts, and teased Briana about her 'thin blood'. She ignored him.

Briana insisted Dad set the heater to full blast as he negotiated his way through the traffic onto the M4. At this time of the year, Tauranga was still in late summer and comfortably warm. Here in London, it was almost freezing, and Briana hated the cold.

Once they made it past the outer edges of London and into the countryside, she held Rashid up to see the little thatched cottages. "Aren't the houses cute?"

Hamish raised his eyebrows. "Briana, stop talking to a stuffed bit of imitation fur. Honestly, it's so embarrassing at your age." Briana was about to bite out a reply, but held her tongue. She was too tired to get into an argument.

They arrived in Abergavenny just before 10.00 am. Briana made Dad stop the car so she could take a photo of Rashid next to a sign saying, 'Welcome to Abergavenny'. After this, they followed the signs to the Tourist Information Centre. Aunty Alys had e-mailed last week to say it would be best for them to get a map and directions from there to Tyn-y-Bryn, the Bed & Breakfast she and Uncle Wynn owned.

Briana walked through the Information Centre doors and froze. Behind the counter was a large, heavily bearded man wearing a badge saying 'Dafydd', and sitting on his desk, smoking a pipe, was the mysterious projected animation of Christopher's Briana had seen on their farm in New Zealand.

II: Strange Happenings

Briana studied the creature carefully. Up close she could see this was not an animation but an animatronic, and the quality was incredible. Although Christopher was only a student, the creature was of a standard even Weta Workshop would be proud of.

"Bree, move out of the way will you?" Hamish pushed his sister out of the doorway. Dad approached the counter, introduced himself to Dafydd (who gently corrected Dad's pronunciation of his name to Dah-vith), and asked for directions to Tyn-y-Bryn.

Briana questioned Hamish. "How did you and Christopher get it here? This is amazing."

Hamish looked innocent enough. "Get what where?"

"The animatronic, the one I thought was a projection back home. Hamish, really, this is very, very high quality, I didn't know Christopher was so good."

"What in hell are you talking about?"

The animatronic spoke to Briana. "No one else can see

me, or hear me, My Lady."

"How is he making it talk?" Briana asked Hamish.

"How is who making what talk?"

"How is Christopher making the animatronic talk?"

Hamish looked at her strangely. "Are you okay?"

Briana was still half-convinced this was some insane prank Hamish, Lachlan, and Christopher had concocted between them. But Mum and Dad wouldn't play along, and they, and Dafydd, didn't seem to be taking any notice of the creature. She frowned, as Hamish declared, "The jet lag has made you whacko," before moving off to look at postcards.

The creature spoke again. "My Lady, you must be at the Abergavenny Markets tomorrow. Meet me at the bookstall at eleven o'clock. Your aunt will know where it is." He clasped his necklace, said what sounded more like 'Riffle out', and disappeared in a puff of green smoke, as he had done in New Zealand. Briana continued to stare at the spot where he'd disappeared, until Mum asked her what was wrong.

"Errr, nothing."

A burst of laughter from Hamish made her turn around, thinking he was finally about to admit to the prank. Instead, he handed her a postcard showing the word 'Llanfairpwll-gwyngyllgogerychwyrndroblllllantysiliogogogoch'. "Wrap your tongue around that, Bree."

Dafydd saw which postcard Briana was holding, and smiled. "Llanfairpwllgwyngyllgogerychwyrndrobwllllantysilio-gogogoch is the name of a village in Wales that translates into English as St. Mary's Church in the hollow of the white hazel near a rapid whirlpool and the Church of St. Tysilio of the red cave." He managed to say all that in one breath.

Dafydd wrote the name out phonetically, and a URL where they could hear it spoken.

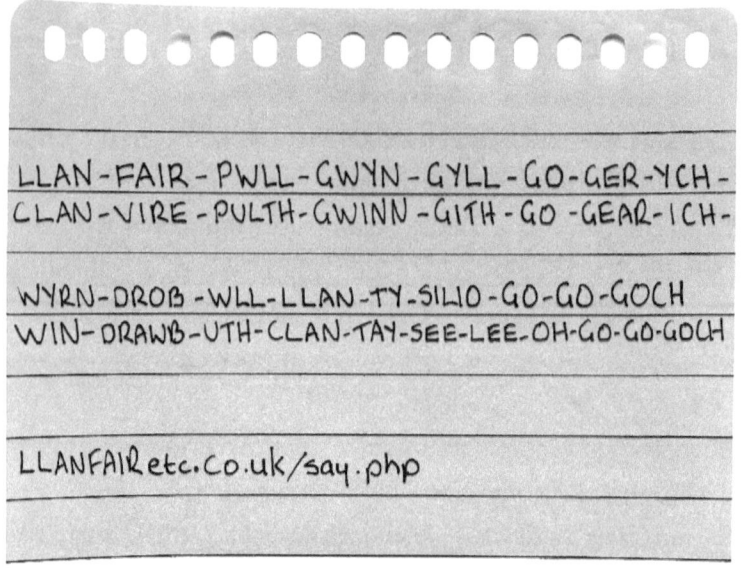

LLAN-FAIR-PWLL-GWYN-GYLL-GO-GER-YCH-
CLAN-VIRE-PULTH-GWINN-GITH-GO-GEAR-ICH-

WYRN-DROB-WLL-LLAN-TY-SILIO-GO-GO-GOCH
WIN-DRAWB-UTH-CLAN-TAY-SEE-LEE-OH-GO-GO-GOCH

LLANFAIRetc.Co.uk/say.php

"Obviously you type the whole name, not 'etc'," he told Briana. "I expect you to be able to say it the next time you come into the Information Centre. He handed the piece of paper to her, and she noted it took two lines for him to write the village name.

Hamish snatched the paper off her. "Wasting your time with her mate, she can't even manage Raxicoricofallapatorius, but I'll master it quickly enough."

"Indeed. Llanfairpwllgwyngyllgogerychwyrndrobwllllantysiliogogogoch shouldn't present too much trouble to someone who can pronounce Raxicoricofallapatorius."

Hamish looked excited. "Are you going to the Convention?"

"Absolutely. And you?"

"That's why I'm here," Hamish replied with a grin.

"You've come to Wales from New Zealand specifically for the Doctor Who Convention? That's dedication."

Hamish laughed. "Not exactly. I didn't really want to come on this trip, I mean, it's a long time without surfing, but the olds insisted." He sighed dramatically. "I tried to point out I'm legally old enough to stay home by myself, but they wouldn't budge. However, I did manage to guilt them a bit and con them into paying for a ticket to the Convention for me, before they found out how much it was."

Briana smiled. Ninety pounds for a ticket. Dad was furious when he found out, but he and Hamish had already shaken hands on the deal and Dad wouldn't go back on his word, even knowing Hamish had conned him. Dad expected it would be the equivalent price of the Armageddon Expos Hamish had been going to in Auckland with Christopher and Lachlan since he was twelve, not over ten times that price.

"How long do you have to wait before you get the shows on television in New Zealand?" Dafydd asked Hamish.

"Oh, the same day on Prime TV now, but I download the episodes straight after transmission in the U.K. otherwise I'd have to stay off social media for hours to avoid spoilers. Hey, what do you think of ..."

Briana, unusually for someone of her age, zoned out as soon as anyone mentioned social media. She left them to it and looked through the rest of the postcards, selecting a few to buy, including one that featured Welsh runes and alphabets from the sixth to tenth centuries. Hamish and his gaming buddies were fascinated with ancient alphabets and used them often. Lachlan would leave notes for Hamish on their front door written in runes invented by Tolkien.

Briana gave the postcard to Hamish. "A present for you."

"Wow, I haven't seen this one before, fantastic. Thanks, Bree. I can use this for Brandaverian."

"Who?"

"One of my gaming characters."

"Oh."

After depleting some of the shop's stock of souvenirs they headed back to the car, taking the little hand-drawn map Dafydd had sketched showing them the route to Tyn-y-Bryn. Dad drove down Monk Street and past St. Mary's Priory Church, where a number of the twins' ancestors were buried. They were descended, on their mother's side, from Owain Glyndŵr, the last Welsh Prince of Wales.

Mum's maiden name was Baker-Gabb and the two families (the Bakers and the Gabbs) had lived in and around Abergavenny for hundreds of years (although the twins' Mum, and even their grandmother, had been born in New Zealand). When they were younger, the friends of both twins thought it was pretty cool their ancestors came from somewhere the Knight Bus stopped at. Last year Hamish and his friends had watched all four seasons of Torchwood in a marathon long weekend session, and Hamish was excited when Abergavenny was mentioned in the second season.

Following Dafydd's instructions Dad turned left at Park Road and right at Pen-Y-Pound Road. Briana was the first to spot half-hidden and overgrown little signs pointing to Tyn-y-Bryn. As the car wound its way up the hill she saw, in paddocks on one side of the road or the other, half a dozen donkeys, as well as two horses, a flock of sheep, and a herd of cows.

The road narrowed so much and the trees leant so far over it gave the illusion of driving through a tunnel. As the trees ended, Briana saw a two-story white farm house with twin chimneys and a rambling rose vine on one side of the entrance. Dad beeped the horn as he drove so Uncle Wynn and Aunty Alys were waiting outside the house to meet them when they arrived.

Uncle Wynn was a tall, grey-haired, stout man with a broad Welsh accent. His large build made him look like Santa Claus, and Briana soon discovered he was equally as jovial. He even laughed with a deep 'ho ho ho'. Aunty Alys was as tall and slender as both her older sister and Briana, and although she had gained a Welsh accent from years of living there, it wasn't as strong as Uncle Wynn's.

Aunty Alys hugged them one after the other. "Welcome, welcome. Oh Isabel, it's been too long, much too long, Tony, it's so good to see you again, and look at the size of you two now, you're both so tall."

Aunty Alys had spent six months in New Zealand after the twins were born, but hadn't been back to see them since. Mum had asked her to come over many times, and arrangements were made over the years, but the plans always fell through. The Ryan's hadn't been able to afford to travel to the U.K. until this year, when the farm finally started making a good profit, so the sisters hadn't seen each other for fifteen years.

As they walked up the slate steps to the house and turned the corner, Briana let out a cry of delight. Three Jack Russell puppies were lying with their mother in a box by the door. Once the parents, Rosy and Busby, had sniffed Briana and

Hamish, they allowed them access to the puppies. After giving them a quick pat Hamish went inside, but Briana stayed with them for a while longer before the lure of seeing Tyn-y-Bryn drew her in.

"It looks exactly like an old Welsh farm-house," she told Hamish as she entered the house, and placed Rashid on the big wooden dining table.

Hamish was chewing the last mouthful of a sandwich. "Maybe that's because it is, genius."

The front door led into the dining room, where the floor and walls were made of slate. A huge fireplace with a magnificent ancient-looking stove filled the entire left-hand wall of the room. Pots, pans, lamps, old saws, farm tools, and horseshoes hung from hooks on the walls.

Hamish waved at a spiral staircase, also made of slate, leading to the second level. "Rooms are up there."

Half-way down the upstairs corridor, Briana found the room she was to share with Hamish (whose suitcase was already dumped on the bed closest to the window). Unlike the dark slate-grey room downstairs, the walls of their bedroom were painted brilliant white, and were decorated with photos of the Welsh countryside. The ceiling slanted from a normal roof level above the door to about a metre above the floor on the opposite wall. Into this were set two huge windows overlooking the valley and the town, and underneath the windows were shelves full of books on Celtic myths and legends.

Hamish entered the room behind Briana and pointed at the view out the window. "Wicked, aye?" He kicked his suitcase off the bed and collapsed dramatically on it.

"I'm knackered. Wake me for lunch, will ya?"

Briana nodded, before heading back down the corridor and the stairs. Pausing halfway, she could hear voices in the kitchen. She recognised Aunty Alys's, but there was also a deep Welsh brogue that, strangely, sounded almost familiar, and a slightly higher-pitched voice. She didn't recognise the language, but presumed it was Welsh.

Taking another step down, she misjudged it, and cried out as she half-fell down a few steps. The voices in the kitchen stopped and Aunty Alys hurried over, wiping her eyes as she came. Briana assured her she was all right, followed her aunt back into the kitchen, and asked who she had been talking to.

Aunty Alys didn't look at her. "Oh, I – I – no one. I had the radio on."

Briana looked into the kitchen, and felt the blood drain from her face. She pointed at a faint puff of green smoke in the middle of the room. "What's that?"

"Why Briana, you've gone white, poor child, the fall must have frightened you; go into the lounge and sit down and I'll make you a nice cup of tea."

"I'm fine, but what is …"

"Come now, dear, that could easily have been a nasty fall, and if it was a result of the effects of jet lag, you could have another turn. Let's get you off your feet, you need to rest." She manoeuvred Briana into the living room, which had the same white-washed walls as the twins' bedroom upstairs. Aunty Alys headed back to the kitchen, but soon reappeared with a cup of tea for Briana.

"Aunty Alys, where did that green smoke come from?"

"What green smoke, dear?"

"That green, oh, nothing." Briana drank her tea as her aunt once again returned to the kitchen. After finishing the tea, she took the empty cup back into the small kitchen and looked around. There was no sign of a radio.

She was about to say something, when her mother came in and started chatting to Aunty Alys. Briana sighed, and went back upstairs to have a lie down, thinking maybe she was suffering from jet lag, or something. Were hallucinations of animatronics and green smoke and hearing voices a side effect of jet lag? She hadn't heard of it before, but maybe, although that wouldn't explain seeing the animatronic in New Zealand.

For the rest of the day they pottered around Tyn-y-Bryn, with the adults catching up on fifteen years of lost time. Briana spent most of her time with the puppies.

Dinner that night was spectacular. Two roast chickens, piles of roast potatoes, pumpkin, carrots, leeks, and onions as well as lots of peas, and gravy all over. For dessert there was an enormous homemade pavlova, with lashings of whipped cream and slices of kiwifruit. ('In case you're homesick already'). Hamish had three large pieces.

After dinner Mum went to bed early. She had a headache again, and was dizzy and drowsy, but fobbed Briana's concerns off with a comment about jet lag. She felt that excuse was wearing thin. Dad saw Mum to bed, then came back downstairs and sat around the dining table with Uncle Wynn and Aunty Alys, drinking coffee.

Hamish asked if he could use the computer. Aunty Alys pointed to a tiny alcove off the dining room. "Of course, it's through there."

Hamish was furious when Mum and Dad had insisted he leave his laptop behind ('You spend far too much time locked in your room on-line, a break will do you good'), but had been slightly mollified when they said he could use the computer at Tyn-y-Bryn.

Briana was about to sit with the adults, when a scream came from the alcove Hamish had walked into. She ran in, the adults close behind her. Hamish was staring at the computer with a look of horror on his face.

"Hamish, what's wrong?" Dad asked.

"No USB drive, no DVD drive, there's only a floppy drive, a floppy for God's sake, I didn't know they even existed anymore, and a DIAL-UP MODEM." Briana and Dad looked at each other, and collapsed in laughter. Hamish glared at them, and looked at Uncle Wynn. "How old is this computer?"

"I can't remember exactly, had it for years, hardly ever use it, don't like those new-fangled things. Alys checks for e-mails for bookings for the B&B every morning, and that's about it. Don't trust the damn things since a friend of ours lost ten thousand pounds to some bloke from Nigeria." The adults went back to the dining table, Dad still laughing. Briana looked at Hamish. "What do you need a computer for? You've got your cell phone."

"Yeah, but I didn't bother to upgrade for international roaming, figuring I could use the computer here for a month instead of paying the rates to use my cell in the U.K. But I never dreamed they'd have such a bloody dinosaur. How can I game with Lachlan and what the hell am I supposed to watch sci-fi on?"

"You don't have your DVDs here to watch. Mum found them in your suitcase and made you take them out before we left."

"Oh pur-lease. No one watches DVDs anymore. Those were the decoys so the olds wouldn't know I brought this." He showed her his external hard drive. "I've done so much surfing lately, on the ocean, not the net, that I'm way behind on *Agents of S.H.I.E.L.D*, *Arrow*, *The Flash*, and *Gotham*, I still have to finish off the last seasons of *Eureka*, *Fringe*, and *Andromeda*, and I haven't even started *Game of Thrones* yet, since I know when I do it will be a season-a-day mission, and I haven't had the time, so there's a few seasons of that too. This sucks big time."

Briana stared at him in disbelief. "When, exactly, were you planning on watching all that? We're only here for a month, you idiot, and we'll be busy doing stuff in the real world most of that time."

As Hamish stomped out of the room Briana laughed to herself. She composed and sent a short general e-mail to her friends ("arrvd safe in aber, shttrd exhorstd, they have puppies!!! goin bed, love you all, will write 2moro"), and then shut the computer down. Laughing again to herself she had to agree Hamish was right, the dial-up was abominably slow. Poor Hamish. No surfing, either on a computer or on the ocean, no gaming, and no sci-fi. She suspected this was going to be a long month for him.

Briana was tired again, so she told the adults she'd turn in for the night. Her aunt took Rashid off her lap, kissed him goodnight, and handed him to Briana. It was strange how Aunty Alys had carried Rashid around all day.

As she entered their room she commented to Hamish, who was busy texting, "It seems weird being dark this early in February. I thought it was too expensive to use your cell?"

"Yeah, just texting the bad news to Lachlan." Hamish finished and threw the phone down, then pointed out the window to the night sky. "That is pretty close to the far end of weird."

"What is?"

"Orion's Belt is upside down, and the Southern Cross ain't there."

Briana looked out. Hamish was right; it was strange to see the night sky looking so different. Taking her pyjamas out of her suitcase, she took Rashid to the bathroom with her while she had a shower and brushed her teeth. She didn't trust Hamish not to chuck him out the window.

After returning to the room she curled up in bed, expecting to fall asleep almost straight away. However, at home, Schrödinger slept on his back lying on her right side between her ribs and her arm, and Einstein slept on her pillow, using Briana's head as his pillow. Briana missed them terribly, and their absence meant it was a long time before she fell asleep.

Unfortunately, having fallen asleep with the light on, she woke when Hamish switched it out just after midnight.

"Bother."

"What?"

"Nothing." Briana rolled over, and tossed and turned for a while before climbing out of bed and opening the door.

"Where are you going?" Hamish asked.

"Toilet," she replied, heading for the bathroom. Walking

past her aunt and uncle's bedroom she could hear Uncle Wynn talking, and there seemed to be an urgent, warning tone in his voice. "You and Caranthir need to be more careful. Briana almost caught you today."

III: Alasdair Toddington

"Briana?" Dad queried, coming out of his room as she stood still, listening outside her Aunt and Uncle's door.

Briana jumped.

Dad laughed. "Sorry, honey, I didn't mean to startle you. What are you doing up?"

"Toilet." She walked down the corridor again.

"Race you." Dad cut in front of her and zipped into the bathroom. Nice to see chivalry is dead over here as well, she thought. Dad grinned at her when he came out, and said goodnight.

Briana closed the bathroom door behind her, her heartbeat still above normal. Who was Caranthir, and what did Briana nearly catch him, or her, doing with Aunty Alys that seemed to concern her uncle so much? After finishing in the bathroom, she headed back to her room, noticing her aunt and uncle's light was now out. After climbing into bed it was a long time before she fell asleep again.

Briana was woken the next morning by the sound of

Hamish in the other bed, carefully reciting, "Clan-vire-pulth-gwinn-gith-go-gear-ich . . ."

"Hamish," she complained sleepily, trying to decide whether to get out of bed or not.

"Clan-vire-pulth-gwinn-gith-go-gear-ich . . ." Briana threw her pillow at him.

"CLAN-VIRE-PULTH-GWINN-GITH-GO-GEAR-ICH-WIN-DRAWB . . ."

Giving up on the hope of any more sleep, Briana went off to the bathroom. When she returned, Hamish had gone, leaving his bed unmade. Briana made hers, and pondered what to wear, as she needed to dress for both fashion and the climate. Yesterday although it had been reasonably warm in the afternoon, she discovered one needed to be well prepared to face a Welsh day in February. Layers was the answer. Many layers.

After dressing and putting on her make-up she went downstairs, where she found Aunty Alys in the kitchen making breakfast. "It's almost ready. Could you go and fetch your uncle and brother for me please?"

"Of course," Briana replied politely, then paused. "Umm, Aunty Alys?"

"Yes dear?"

"Who's . . . umm, I mean, where are they?" She decided at the last instant not to raise the issue of what she had heard Uncle Wynn say last night.

Aunty Alys pointed out the kitchen window to the right. "Walk down the steps, follow the garden path there, walk past the bushes, and you'll find them in the stone cottage. You can leave Rashid here, I'll look after him."

"Oh, okay." Briana handed him over, but wondered again about her Aunt's strange fondness for the toy monkey.

Following Aunty Alys's instructions, Briana soon reached the little stone cottage that was available for visitors who wanted more privacy than a B&B offered. Inside, Uncle Wynn lay on some scaffolding painting the ceiling, while Hamish stirred a paint pot. Uncle Wynn rubbed his neck as he came down from the scaffolding, and seemed glad to stop what he was doing.

After breakfast the twins, their parents, and Aunty Alys (and Rashid) drove into town, leaving Uncle Wynn behind to work on the cottage again. They parked at the Information Centre and went inside, where Dafydd was on duty again. As Hamish walked in, he announced, "Llanfairpwllgwyngyllgo-gerychwyrndrobwllllantysiliogogogoch."

"Oh well done, lad," Dafydd beamed. "That fully entitles you to this." He gave Hamish a key ring with a picture of the Welsh flag on one side, and on the other side:

TO BE BORN WELSH

To be born Welsh
is to be born privileged.
Not with a silver spoon
in your mouth,
but music in your blood
and poetry in your soul.

"Cool, thanks."

"You're welcome." Dafydd hesitated. "Why do you have 'Fetid Cat Drool' written on your T-shirt?"

Hamish informed him it was one of his favourite bands.

"Can't say I've heard of them."

"No, you wouldn't have, they're from our high school back home in New Zealand. Last year they won a national band competition, and landed a recording contract, and they're huge on YouTube, but old people don't like them."

"What sort of music do they play?" Dafydd asked, ignoring, Briana noted, Hamish's jibe about 'old people'.

"Rubbish," Briana commented before Hamish spoke.

Hamish gave her a withering look. "The Cats are a five-piece band who play heavy metal. The singer, the guitarist, and the drummer also have a separate three-piece band who play hard rock."

"Dare I ask what they're called?"

Hamish grinned. "Rancid Dog Slobber."

Dafydd laughed. "I knew I shouldn't have asked." He looked at Briana. "What about you, lass, who are your favourite bands? I always enjoy finding out what kids are listening to these days, 'old' as I may look to you."

"She doesn't listen to anyone normal people have heard of," Hamish replied, getting back at Briana. "Or, at least, normal people our age."

Briana frowned slightly, knowing Hamish had a point. Her friends were all crazy about bands and singers Hamish deprecatingly called 'sugar pop'. Briana's taste in music, however, ran to bands that, as Hamish said, most people their age hadn't heard of, such as Lo Còr De La Plana, Babylon Circus, Ozomatli, and Nakho & Medicine for the People. And while her friends spent hours listening to whoever was the latest chart breaking singer, Briana would be listening to Xavier Rudd, Salif Keita, and David D'Or. Some of her parents' friends, who had been to WOMAD festivals, knew who these artists were, and always praised Briana for her 'adult and eclectic' taste in music, but Briana's friends all thought she was a bit mental.

She didn't even know how she stumbled onto these bands. Every so often she would sit at her computer, open YouTube, and type a name which meant nothing to her as she typed. But invariably the video would be of a musician or band, and when they started playing, Briana wouldn't only hear the music with her ears, she would hear it with her soul. The music moved her in ways she couldn't explain.

"I, umm, I listen to different music." Briana didn't elaborate, instead she moved off to have another look through the souvenirs. Hamish spent another ten minutes chatting about sci-fi and fantasy with Dafydd, after which they left and walked up Cross Street on their way to St. Mary's Priory Church.

"Monk Street," Hamish announced at the corner. "Down here, Aunty Alys?"

From reading the website earlier Briana knew St. Mary's was considered one of the most fascinating medieval churches in Wales, and was home to one of the world's finest medieval wood sculptures, the Jesse Carving.

According to the website, the priory was established at the end of the eleventh century by the Norman lord Hamelin de Ballon, to support a prior and twelve monks from the French Abbey of St. Vincent and St. Lawrence in Le Mans. Little of the original building remained, but most of the existing building still dated back to the fourteenth century. Hundreds of years of history was alive in the air around her as she walked slowly toward the back of the church.

She wandered around looking at the monuments, tombs, memorials, and figures carved from alabaster and wood. Aunty Alys pointed out the tomb of one of the twins' ancestors, William Baker, and his wife Joan, and showed Briana where some of their other ancestors, Thomas Gabb, Baker Gabb Esq., and John Gabb, were entombed in the floor. Briana tried not to walk on them.

Looking around she saw Hamish was busy taking photos of all the monuments on his cell phone, probably to use in his gaming back home. What would their ancestors from hundreds of years ago think if they could see what Hamish would do with their images on his computer?

One of the items that impressed Briana the most was the Abergavenny Tapestry, a magnificent work twenty-four feet long (according to the plaque) created by sixty volunteers over six years.

Briana had tried a small tapestry of Winnie the Pooh when she was younger, and had given up after only a few hours. This tapestry had taken twenty thousand hours of work, was designed to celebrate one thousand years of Abergavenny history, and included a depiction of Owain Glyndŵr. It was a strangely emotional experience to look upon the image of her ultimate grand-father.

Once everyone had finished looking at (and photo-graphing) everything they wanted to, they headed back outside, stopping to sign the Visitors' Book on the way.

"Where to now?" Hamish asked Aunty Alys. "Can we go and see the castle?"

Glancing at her watch Briana was about to recommend heading to the Markets as it was getting close to 11.00 a.m.

when her aunt suggested it. Briana decided to push a bit. "I'd rather go to the castle first; we can go to the Markets afterward."

Aunty Alys looked at her own watch. "No, it would be best to go to the Markets first."

Briana pushed further. "Why? What's so urgent we have to go there now?"

"Nothing, dear, but many stalls sell out early."

Briana remained suspicious, but didn't say anything else.

At Market Hall they found dozens of stalls, with stall keepers loudly bawling their wares in a variety of British accents. Briana bought six little ceramic dragons for herself and a Welsh bandana for Rashid, which she tied around his neck.

Hamish bought himself a Union Jack T-shirt, which he put on over the top of his Fetid Cat Drool one. He asked the stall keeper if he could come and stand behind the stall with him, and asked Briana to take a photo of them on his phone.

"Tourist," Briana teased him, looking at the T-shirt.

Hamish snorted. "Says she who's bought the Welsh equivalent of plastic tikis, which were probably made in China. Besides, if the T-shirt is good enough for Rose, it's good enough for me."

"Who's Rose?"

"Never mind."

Briana took the photo, handed his phone back to him, and then took some of her own photos on her digital camera. She preferred to keep her phone for phoning and her camera for photos. Hamish always had a late-model phone, which he acquired cheaply through contacts of Christopher's. Briana wasn't fussed with smartphones, preferring to talk to people in person, and her old flip-phone got two weeks of battery life compared to Hamish's day (if he was lucky).

As Hamish walked toward the next stall, Briana turned over one of the dragons and saw a little sticker: 'Made in China'. "Bother," she muttered under her breath. Peeling all the stickers off, she surreptitiously placed them in the nearest rubbish bin. As she caught up with Hamish she heard him ask, "Mum, can I meet you in an hour? I don't really want to get dragged around looking at girlie stuff with you ladies."

Dad laughed. "Well, I wouldn't have put it like that, at least not to her face." He smiled at Mum. "It's a good idea though, I'll head off separately too. I have a list of things Wynn asked me to pick up. What say we all meet back at the front entrance in an hour?" He pointed at Hamish. "And you, be on time or you can walk home." Hamish grinned at him and vanished into the crowds, and then Dad headed off after Aunty Alys set him in the right direction.

"Bree, do you want to go off by yourself too?" Mum asked.

"That depends. What sort of stalls are you interested in looking at?"

Aunty Alys indicated with a gesture of her head. "There's a great second-hand book stall I like to have a browse through whenever I'm here."

Briana looked sharply at her aunt. "Why do you want us to go to a book stall?" she asked.

"Don't you and Isabel both love books?"

Briana had to agree. "We do."

"There you go. We don't have to if you don't want to."

Briana looked at her watch. "No, it's okay, we'll go there."

Aunty Alys led them through the hall, outside, and down some steps toward the book stall. Once there, Aunty Alys ferreted through the cookbooks. Mum, who taught Classical Studies at Tauriko College where the twins went to school, searched for books on ancient Greece or Rome.

Briana placed Rashid on the table, and looked for books on nature or science. She wasn't a big reader of fiction, unless it was something like the 1991 classic *Sophie's World* by Jostein Gaarder.

She was flicking through a fascinating book on insects when something touched her ankle. Glancing down she saw a gnarled hand, so she crouched and looked under the table. The mysterious creature was sitting there cross-legged with an enormous book on his lap.

"Lady Briana, my name is Alasdair Toddington and I am the Keeper of the Atlas. Please forgive my unorthodox method of introduction. I had planned to give the Atlas to you on your sixteenth birthday, but doing so here will provide you with an excuse to tell your parents where it came from, and it's close enough to your birthday."

He passed the book to an astonished Briana, clasped his necklace, said "Riffle out," (it was definitely 'riffle' and not 'ripple' Briana noted) and disappeared, leaving behind a puff of green smoke.

"I'm going completely mad," Briana muttered to Rashid, before standing and placing the book on the table.

The book was heavy, looked to be incredibly old, and was bound in thick leather. The solid book in Briana's hands caused a shiver to run down her. Until now, when seeing this … what had he said his name was? Oh yes, when seeing this

Alasdair Toddington, Briana could still convince herself she was hallucinating, or it was a side effect of jet lag, or something. Anything. But this, this was real! This book she could touch, and she had felt Alasdair's hand on her ankle.

Turning the cover of the book, she discovered pages and pages of runes and beautifully coloured 'olde worlde' style maps.

Mum looked over Briana's shoulder. "Impressive."

So, although no one else had been able to see Alasdair, obviously Mum could at least see the book he'd given Briana.

"It must be worth a fortune, Bree."

"Won't know until I've asked. Excuse me, how much is this book?"

The stall keeper looked at it. "Well now, where did that come from? It's not one of mine. I've never seen it before."

Aunty Alys placed a hand on the woman's arm. "Are you sure, dear?"

The stall keeper's eyes glazed over and her voice changed to a dull monotone, "Oh, yes, five pounds please."

"Five pounds? For this? Surely it must be worth more than that? Twenty pounds at least."

"Mum, you're supposed to bargain down, not up."

"Well, yes, but, oh, are you sure?" Mum asked the woman.

Speaking in the same dull monotone, the stall keeper replied, "Five pounds."

"Sold." Briana deposited five pounds in the woman's hand.

Aunty Alys took her hand off the woman's arm, who blinked her eyes, shook her head and seemed to look in surprise at the money in her hand.

Briana was about to say something when she heard Dad's voice. "Alys, I can't find everything on Wynn's list. Any ideas?"

Approaching from the opposite direction he'd left in, he handed the list over to Aunty Alys, who scanned it quickly. "I don't think anything on here was urgent. Wynn can pop into town later and collect what's missing from Richards of Abergavenny. I'm sure he'll be glad to get away. Painting is not his favourite job."

Briana followed behind the adults as they went looking for Hamish (who hadn't come back when he was supposed to). But really, she had lost all interest in the market by this stage, and wished for nothing more than to get back to Tyn-y-Bryn to investigate this wonderful and mysterious old Atlas.

The book in her hands had finally silenced the small part of her mind that had been stubbornly trying to deny Alasdair's existence, and she hoped to find some more clues as to who, and what, he was in the ancient pages.

IV: A Knight in the Night

Briana detected a jealous gleam in Hamish's eye as he browsed through her book. The family, after locating the errant Hamish, had made their way to the King's Arms pub for lunch, and Hamish was impressively blown away by the book. "Wow, it's fantastic! Bree, this is amazingly and totally awesome, and the paper is so thick and looks hand-made, it could be centuries old."

"Can you read it?"

Hamish shook his head. "No. I mean, a few runes look similar to Tolkien's, but that might be coincidence. And even if I can find out what the runes are, they might not translate into English. It could be in Welsh. Do you speak Welsh, Aunty Alys?"

She laughed. "I might have lived here for twenty years, but I only speak a few words. Your Uncle Wynn is fluent, though. He grew up on a remote farm outside Gwynedd and didn't learn English until he was ten."

If that was true, what was the language Briana had heard

in the kitchen? Coming, Aunty Alys had said, from a radio. That didn't exist.

Hamish looked up as the waiter approached their table. "Sweet, if it's Welsh we can ask him. I'll have the hot peppered fillet and pate of smoked mackerel, hold the anchovy sticks, with the toast, hold the horseradish cream for a starter, followed by the beer battered fillet of cod, crushed peas if they have to be crushed, but if you have them unsquashed I'd prefer them whole, hand-cut chips, if I could have a few extra of those that'd be sweet, can I have tomato sauce instead of the tartare sauce, and a Coke." Briana rolled her eyes at him.

"What?"

"You took so long to order the kitchen has closed."

The waiter smiled at her. "My Lady?"

"Why did you call me that?" Her tone was sharp as recognised the term of address Alasdair Toddington used for her.

"Briana, don't be rude."

"I'm not, Dad, it's just, just ..."

"What?"

"Nothing, sorry."

Hamish shook his head at the waiter. "Don't worry about her, she's my twin – I kicked her in the head on the way out, and she's never been the same since."

"That's enough Hamish."

"It's fine Dad." Briana looked at the menu. "I'll have the trout thanks, and an orange juice." She had been surprised to see trout on the menu, until Dad told her New Zealand was probably the only country in the world where it was illegal to buy or sell trout. You could only cook and eat trout you'd caught yourself. Briana was determined to make the most of it while they were in Wales.

Mum was, once again, looking pale, and Briana noticed her hands were trembling slightly. "Are you okay?"

Mum folded her hands in her lap. "I'm fine, honey, a touch of jet lag still, I think."

Briana exchanged a glance with Hamish. Yeah, right, Briana thought, and knew her brother was thinking the same thing. Hamish looked like he was about to say something, so Briana shook her head slightly. She knew if there was something seriously wrong with Mum, she would try to hide it from them, so there was no point in pursuing the matter with her.

The twins sat side by side at a separate table, which was nearly covered by the open book. The left-hand pages were covered in the strange runes, while the right-hand pages had the maps. They were extremely detailed, coloured in pale greens, blues, and browns, and each page seemed to be for one country. Border lines were drawn in red, and a glimpse of surrounding countries, where applicable, could be seen at the edges of the pages. In the bottom-left corner of each page was a flag representing the country, while in the opposite corner was a picture of a red dragon, the one seen on the Welsh flag.

Briana pointed to one of the dragons. "The book must have been made here, in Wales. The red dragon must indicate the book's country of origin, surely."

"Maybe. But look here, this is strange."

"What is?"

Hamish tapped the map. "This here, this is Libya, but these are the present-day borders, and they weren't changed until 1934, when British Sudan ceded northern territory to Libya, so it's not going to be hundreds of years old; it can't be more than about eighty years old at the most."

Briana wasn't surprised at her brother's detailed geographical knowledge. He came top of every geography test, and used the knowledge to help him design on-line fantasy gaming lands based on the real world.

Hamish turned a few more pages. "And look at this. The boundary between North Korea and South Korea wasn't established until 1953, along the cease-fire line of the previous 38th parallel."

Hamish turned several more pages. "Oh, no way. Look at the Kosovo and Serbian borders. These date from 2008."

"So, you're telling me this book isn't more than seven years old?"

"It can't be, Bree."

"But it looks so ancient, and the paper is so thick, and the maps are so old-fashioned, it must be hundreds of years old."

Hamish shook his head. "I'm sorry Bree, but it's been made very recently." He closed the book and looked at it. "It's good though. I'd love to know who made it, and why they gave it away at a book sale. Man, I bet the dude who made this wouldn't have any trouble getting a job at Weta Workshop."

Briana didn't say anything. What could she say? The book hadn't been given away in a book sale, but had been given to her by an impossible creature who appeared and disappeared in green smoke? She still hardly believed it herself.

The family had planned to go to Abergavenny Castle after lunch, but with Mum pleading jet lag sick, and the twins keen to examine the book some more (although Hamish not so enthusiastically now he knew the book was 'a fake'), Dad suggested skipping the castle for today. They headed back to Tyn-y-Bryn.

Once there, Briana dropped the book on her bed in their room and sat cross-legged in front of it with Rashid on her lap. Hamish sat next to her as she opened the book and studied the inside front cover.

Carved into the leather were ten lines of identical runes and on the left of each line was one of the little symbols of a red dragon.

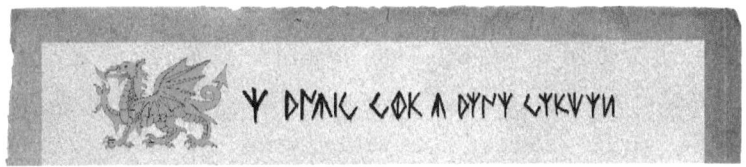

The twins had been staring at the runes for a while in silence, when Hamish declared in an excited voice, "Oh my God, idiot!"

"I am not an idiot."

"Not you, me." He jumped off the bed and scrambled for his backpack. "I knew I recognised them." Pulling out the bag of souvenirs he had bought the day before at the Information Centre, he upended it on the bed. He picked out the postcard of ancient Welsh runes and alphabets, and passed it to Briana. The main image showed *Y Wyddor The Alphabet*, while at the bottom of the postcard were the *Bethluisnion (Ogham Alphabet)* and the *Coelbren Y Beirdd*.

Hamish held the postcard directly under the line of runes

in the Atlas. "Look, these runes are from the *Coelbren Y Beirdd*. Have you got a pen and paper?"

Briana found what he needed in her suitcase.

As she watched, Hamish translated the runes using the postcard. The line read *Y DDRAIG GOCH A DDYRY GYCHWYN*. He also translated the runes on the front cover, *Y LLYFR MAPIAU* and *GYFRWNG MYNEDIAD IR BYD*.

Briana considered the words. "It looks Welsh, it has those double Ls and double Ds, and more unpronounceable words than German."

Hamish laughed.

"What's so funny?"

"Double Ds."

"Oh grow up, Hamish. Let's go and ask Uncle Wynn what it says."

The twins walked to the cottage, where they found Uncle Wynn sitting on a paint tin drinking coffee from a thermos.

Hamish handed him the translations. "Can you please tell us what this says?"

Uncle Wynn held the paper out in front of him and squinted at it. "Nope. Hang on a minute." He went to his toolbox and took out a pair of reading glasses. "That's better. Okay, this line says *y ddraig goch a ddyry gychwyn*, this says *y llyfr mapiau*, and this says *gyfrwng mynediad ir byd*."

"Err, we meant can you tell us what it is in English?" Hamish clarified.

"Oh, of course, sorry. The first bit says, 'the red dragon will show the way', this says 'the Atlas', and this says 'the gateway to the world'. Those words about the red dragon are often affiliated with the red dragon on the Welsh flag. Where did you find them?"

"In that book I bought at the market. It's written in the coal bren ee bed and Hamish translated it from a postcard."

Uncle Wynn laughed his deep ho ho ho. "Your pronunciation is an insult, lass, to the Welsh blood in your veins. The *Coelbren Y Beirdd*, you say? That's strange. It's an old alphabet, but I've never heard of any books written in it."

"Well, I guess there's one at least. Can you translate the rest into English once Hamish has translated the runes?"

"Of course."

"Great, thanks." The twins ran back to their room, where Hamish rewrote the little runes from the postcard in large letters, to make them easier to follow.

After Hamish finished translating the first page of runes, the twins went back to the cottage and gave the page of runic translations to Uncle Wynn.

"Are you sure you've translated them correctly? Into Welsh, I mean."

"Absolutely," Hamish replied, "Why? Doesn't it make sense?"

"Well, no. It's gobbledygook. Nonsense. It's, well, sort of made-up words. It's hard to translate, but it would be like saying in English squiggle wiggle waffle dippity woof blurf."

Briana laughed.

"The whole page?" Hamish asked, frowning at Briana.

"I'm afraid so, lad."

Hamish checked his translations, and insisted they were correct. Briana suggested maybe it wasn't the *Coelbren Y Beirdd* after all. Hamish argued the runes in the book and on the postcard were such a perfect match, and the line about the Red Dragon showing the way had made sense. It was strange. He tried the next page of runes, but when he took the translation to Uncle Wynn, he was told it was still gobbledygook.

Briana watched Hamish throw down the translations in frustration. "Ah, if only Dumbledore were here."

"What?"

"Doesn't he speak gobbledygook?"

"Oh funny ha ha. I thought you didn't read fiction?"

"We had to read *Harry Potter* for English," she reminded him.

"Quite right too," he replied with a grin.

Briana was confused about the runes, but not too upset,

while Hamish took the failure hard. He tried his translations again, while Briana went outside to play with the puppies.

That night she wrote a longer e-mail to her friends telling them what she'd been doing. However, she didn't, for some reason, mention the book to them. She was about to hit send when Dad came in. "Who are you writing to, honey?"

"Oh, just sending a general e-mail to everyone back home," Briana replied.

"Have you included Cheryl?"

"I don't want to write to her."

"Honestly, Briana, I don't know why you don't like her, she's a lovely girl. Look, I told David we'd keep them up to date with what we're doing here, but he doesn't have an e-mail address, so you'll have to e-mail Cheryl."

"That cow's not going to be interested in what I've been doing."

"Briana Rose Alys Ryan."

"Sorry," Briana apologised insincerely. "I can't e-mail her anyway, I don't know her address."

"I asked her for it before we left."

"Oh, goody." Briana added the address in as Dad dictated it, intending to delete it before hitting send. Dad's eyes bored into her back. "Fine." She hit send.

Briana went to bed early, and fell asleep soon after lying down. On waking the following morning she found out Hamish had stayed up late working with the runes and a Welsh-English dictionary, trying to make head or tail of any of the other runes in the book, but without any further success.

After breakfast the family headed off to the Dan-yr-Ogof

Showcaves near Abercrave, not far from Abergavenny. Briana kept everyone waiting for an hour while she changed, and changed, and changed again, and put on her make-up.

Hamish wanted to take the Atlas with them, even though Aunty Alys said they would get carsick if they tried to read it, and would be too busy at Dan-yr-Ogof to have time to read anyway. When Hamish insisted on taking it, Aunty Alys offered to carry the book to the car.

"I can manage, thanks." His aunt, however, firmly took it out of his hands, and headed toward the car. Briana could hear Aunty Alys muttering as she walked, but couldn't make out the words. At the car, she touched it with one hand, and continued to mutter, before placing the book on the back seat.

"What was that all about, Aunty Alys?" Briana asked.

"Just singing, dear."

Unfortunately Aunty Alys's prediction came true, and within minutes of leaving Tyn-y-Bryn the twins were queasy from trying to read in the car. Hamish reluctantly put the book over the back seat into the trunk of the rental.

They had a great day at the Showcaves, which also featured a dinosaur park with life-size replicas. "Brontosaurus and stegosaurus and iguanodon and tyrannosaurus," Briana pointed out to her parents. She could identify each one before they were close enough to read the signs.

The twins had both been crazy about dinosaurs at a young age, and although Hamish had transferred his obsessions to sci-fi and fantasy as he grew older, Briana was still fascinated by them. She had watched the BBC series *Walking with Dinosaurs* at least a dozen times on DVD, had seen the live show in Auckland in 2011, and had many books about dinosaurs back home. She even owned every season of *Primeval* on DVD, her only concession to watching a 'fantasy' television show.

Hamish was most impressed with the Bone Cave, which contained Roman remains, a Bronze Age family reconstruction, statues of wolves and bears, and, Hamish's favourite, a burial scene.

Briana's favourite was Cathedral Cave, which had a massively spectacular passage, a gorge-like section formed by river action over thousands of years, and the Dome of St. Paul's, a huge chamber with an underground lake fed by two waterfalls about four stories high. The Cathedral Cave also featured cave paintings by an artist who lived twenty thousand years ago. Briana surreptitiously collected a few small samples of rocks to take back to New Zealand for her friend Roanna, who was planning to study geomorphology after high school.

Back outside the caves, Hamish took about a hundred photos of the life-size models of the huts of an Iron Age village. He shot them from every possible angle so he could input them into his computer at home to create a gaming village.

Mum took photos of the twins swinging from the tusks of a woolly mammoth on Hamish's cell phone and Briana's camera. Briana and Mum then headed for the Shire Horse Centre, while Dad and Hamish went off to the go-cart track.

Before leaving Dan-yr-Ogof, the twins managed to talk their parents into buying lots of souvenirs, including plastic dinosaurs, stickers, magnets, and a Dan-yr-Ogof T-shirt each, which was far more satisfying than having to use their own money.

As they headed back to the car in the late afternoon, the twins walked ahead of their parents, chatting about their day, when the peace of the Welsh countryside was shattered by a car alarm.

"What the hell?" Hamish called out.

Briana looked ahead. There was a strange man trying to break into their rental car. He was exceptionally tall, but his height wasn't what made him stand out. He was dressed in the armour of a medieval knight, with the unusual addition of a flowing purple cape.

As Briana watched, he placed both hands on the car's hatch, which opened as he lifted his hands up. After reaching into the interior of the car he let out a scream of pain, and jerked his hands back out.

Hamish grabbed a large stick lying alongside the path and ran toward the car, yelling and shouting, with Dad calling behind him, 'Hamish, no!' The knight looked from the screeching car to Hamish, turned, and ran along the line of parked cars before ducking behind a bushy tree. Hamish followed . . . and stopped. There was no sign of the knight anywhere.

Hamish brushed aside some purple smoke, and looked around. "What the . . . ? He can't have . . . how did he . . . WHERE DID HE GO?" He started running along the rows of parked cars, checking under them, but the knight had vanished completely. The silence as Dad deactivated the alarm was eerie. "What happened, Hamish?"

"Someone tried to break into the car. There must have

been a re-enactment on somewhere today, or a Renaissance Fair or something. I scared him off, but damn, that was pretty close to the far end of weird, and I have no idea what happened to him, it's like he vanished into thin air. Bree, did you see where he went?"

Briana was staring at a plume of purple smoke drifting lazily upward.

"Bree, did you see where he went?" Hamish asked her again.

She continued to stare upward. "Can you see that smoke?"

"Of course I can see it. Did you see where the knight went to?"

"He dissolved into that smoke."

Hamish gave her the look he always gave her when she teased him about being obsessed with sci-fi.

"I'm not . . ." Briana stopped. How could she explain?

Dad examined the hatch. "I hope he hasn't damaged the lock. The petrol prices over here are enough to bankrupt us, without having to pay for damage to the car as well." Looking the hatch over, he closed it and reopened it with the key a couple of times. "That's strange."

"What is?" Mum asked.

Dad scratched his head. "Well, he had the hatch open, but he doesn't seem to have jimmied the lock at all. How did he break in? At least there doesn't seem to be any harm done."

"But where did he go?" Hamish demanded.

Dad looked along the line of parked vehicles, and pointed at a VW Kombi van. "My guess is there. If he was at a re-enactment he's probably been drinking all day, so I'm sure it's all a harmless prank" He shrugged it off as such. "Come on.

We'd better get going or we'll be late back for dinner."

Briana was quiet on the way back to Tyn-y-Bryn. She wondered if the medieval knight was connected with Alasdair Toddington. The knight had disappeared into purple smoke, despite what Dad said, and Alasdair disappeared in green smoke. Surely they had to be connected somehow? She shook her head. Alasdair Toddington. The mysterious book. And now this.

Should she mention Alasdair to Hamish? Now he had seen the knight, and the book Alasdair had given her, maybe he would believe her if she told him the whole story. Then again, he would probably rationalise the knight as being a man in costume, and say again that although the book was impressive, it was nothing more than something that could have been made by Weta Workshop. Briana sighed, and decided to hold her tongue for now.

After dinner, and after Briana had sent another group e-mail home telling everyone about Dan-yr-Ogof, the twins went to their room. Briana decided to break her silence and told Hamish everything about Alasdair Toddington. She also suggested Alasdair and the book might be connected to the knight.

"You're winding me up."

"Damn it, Hamish, I don't believe in all that sci-fi fantasy rubbish, but I haven't teased you about it for a long time now, and I'm not making this up. And even if I was, where did that strange knight come from today? And, more importantly, where did he go? You know he didn't have time to get into the Kombi."

"Bree, much as I would love it if the Doctor arrived and

took me off on a trip in the blue box, or if Luke came and told me I'd been accepted to train as a Jedi Knight, it's not going to happen, is it now? Look, I'm the first to admit I'm obsessed with sci-fi, but I do know the difference between fantasy and reality."

"Well where did that knight disappear to?"

"I don't know, but, but . . ." he snapped his fingers. "Bloody hell, the tree, of course."

"What tree?"

"The tree at the car park, you know, the one that looked like a fat giant candle flame? What are they called?"

"Sorry, I don't know."

"You know the one I mean though? That bushy, massive one. Oh, yeah, cypress tree. He must have hidden in there."

Briana shook her head. "He didn't hide in the tree, Hamish."

"Well, where did he go then? He didn't disappear into thin air in a puff of smoke."

"Yes he did, and you saw the smoke."

"I saw smoke, yes, something from a joke shop, no doubt. But I don't believe he disappeared into thin air. He hid in the tree."

"He did not hide in the tree," Briana insisted, "he disappeared in purple smoke."

"What's going on here? Have we switched bodies or something? You're the realist in the family."

"Hamish, the knight did vanish into thin air and therefore he is probably connected to Alasdair Toddington. He disappears in puffs of smoke too, although it's green smoke."

Hamish shook his head. "Bree, you said you haven't teased

me about sci-fi for a long time, so why start again? I'm too old to be bothered by it now, anyway, so you're wasting your breath. I'm going downstairs to get a glass of water. Want one?"

"No thank you."

After Hamish left, Briana sighed, changed into her pyjamas, and crawled into bed, hugging her monkey tightly. "Something really, really strange is going on, Rashid." When Hamish came back she pretended to be asleep, and didn't notice when she did fall asleep.

Hours later, Briana woke up. She lay there in the dark, not sure what had wakened her. Glancing at her bedside clock she saw it was 3.16 a.m. There was the noise again; a soft metallic clinking. She turned her head to the other side of the room, and screamed.

The medieval knight from Dan-yr-Ogof was bending over her, outlined by the light of the full moon and surrounded by a cloud of purple smoke.

V: The Key to the Atlas

Briana screamed again. Busby, who was sleeping in Aunty Alys and Uncle Wynn's room, barked furiously, echoed a moment later by Rosy, who was downstairs with the puppies. Sitting bolt upright in bed Hamish saw the man and started yelling too.

"Dad, there's a man in here, Dad, Dad, Daaaaaaaaaaad!"

The knight straightened and tried to pick up the Atlas from Briana's bedside table. As soon as his gauntlets touched the book it flashed with a golden fire, causing the knight to drop it with a cry. He fell to the floor with a great clatter as Hamish hit him from behind with a backpack.

Briana could hear footsteps from outside running toward the bedroom, and then Aunty Alys and Uncle Wynn burst through the door. The knight's eyes widened as he looked intently at them, he said something Briana couldn't understand, and disappeared in a puff of purple smoke.

Mum and Dad rushed in, everyone started talking at once, and Busby sniffed everywhere and barked loudly. Mum went to Briana and held her tightly as Briana shook in her arms, sobbing. Mum said soothing things to her, and eventually she calmed down. She wiped her eyes and tried to explain what had happened. Mum and Dad, of course, didn't believe the knight from Dan-yr-Ogof had been in the room, and had vanished in a puff of purple smoke. They told Briana she'd had a nightmare.

"But I saw him too," Hamish protested, "and so did Aunty Alys and Uncle Wynn."

Mum looked at her sister. "Alys?"

Aunty Alys shook her head. "I'm sorry, I didn't see anything. You're right, Briana had a nightmare."

Hamish and Briana were both surprised at this.

"What? You saw him. You both saw him." Hamish looked at Uncle Wynn. "And he saw you. He spoke to you and vanished in purple smoke when he saw you."

"Hamish, that's enough," Dad said. "Don't tease your sister. She's had a bad enough fright from her nightmare."

Briana looked at Busby, who was growling and sniffing the area of carpet where the knight had stood. The dog obviously knew the knight had been here as his fur was still standing on end. Aunty Alys laid a hand on Busby, and quietly murmured something. Busby calmed at her words, curled up with his nose touching his tail, and went to sleep on the floor.

Briana looked at her aunt. "You said you didn't speak Welsh.

"I said I spoke a few words, dear," she replied, not looking at Briana. "It seems to calm the dogs when they're upset. Now, I'll pop downstairs and make us all a nice cup of tea." She left the room, taking Uncle Wynn with her, and saying something to him Briana couldn't quite catch.

Briana rolled her eyes. "A cup of tea? The great British answer to everything. What the hell is that going to solve?"

"Well, if it's good enough to get the Doctor back on his feet after a regeneration."

"Hamish, stop it. Briana, language. A cup of tea is an excellent idea, it's very calming." Mum took Briana by the hand and half-led, half-dragged her downstairs.

When they were all seated around the dining table drinking tea, Uncle Wynn and Aunty Alys again insisted they hadn't seen anything, and Mum and Dad again insisted Briana had had a nightmare. Briana and Hamish escaped as soon as possible and headed back upstairs to their room.

Briana shut the door. "Now do you believe me? You saw the knight? You saw him disappear? In purple smoke? So now do you believe I was telling the truth about his disappearing at Dan-yr-Ogof?"

"It looks like it."

"So, if you believe me about the knight, you have to believe I'm telling the truth about Alasdair as well."

"Bree, I don't know what's going on or why Aunty Alys lied to Mum, and I want to believe you, but it's all way, way past the far end of weird."

"There's been some other weird stuff happening too."

"Such as?"

Briana told Hamish about how she'd heard voices in the kitchen Aunty Alys said came from a radio that didn't exist, and of the green smoke she'd seen, that Aunty Alys had denied, and of the weird thing that had happened with the lady at the book stall where Briana had bought the book.

However, despite Hamish's love of sci-fi, he stubbornly insisted there was all some sort of logical explanation for everything. "It's some clever trick. Criss Angel or Dynamo could easily pull off something like this." He held his hand up as Briana started to object.

"I know, I know, I'm just saying. And I don't have any better idea than you do as to who's done this or what it all means."

He bent down, picked the book up from where it had fallen on the floor, and placed it on Briana's bed, settling himself cross-legged in front of it. Briana sat opposite him, with Rashid on her lap, itching to say something else, but holding her tongue for now.

The twins half-expected the Atlas to do something, but it didn't. It just sat there. Hamish opened it and flicked through it, ending on the blank back page with the cover open. He idly tapped his fingers down the cover. "Well, there must be something important enough about this book that . . ."

Tap, tap, tap, tap, thud.

Briana could hear the distinctly different tone as Hamish tapped the bottom right-hand corner of the book's cover. "It sounds hollow." She pointed to where the paper had lifted the tiniest bit in the corner. "Hamish, look." Briana pulled the paper back and was surprised to hear a noise like pulling Velcro apart.

Lying in an indent in the leather cover was a large gold key. Briana took it out. Hamish grabbed the book, turned it face up toward Briana, and pointed to the keyhole on the front. "Try it in here."

"This key is far too long to fit in there."

"Just try it, Bree." He grinned at her. "Maybe it's bigger on the inside." Even Briana knew what that referred to.

She inserted the key, and gasped as the entire length of it slid into the keyhole. She opened the cover, but there was no sign of the key poking through. She closed it. "How strange. Now what?"

"D'uh, genius. Turn . . . the . . . key."

Briana narrowed her eyes at him but did as she was told. The cover slowly opened by itself, and red, blue, and green smoke issued from the book.

As Briana watched in amazement, the runes on the inside of the front cover changed. There were still ten lines of runes, but each was different now. She studied the first four lines.

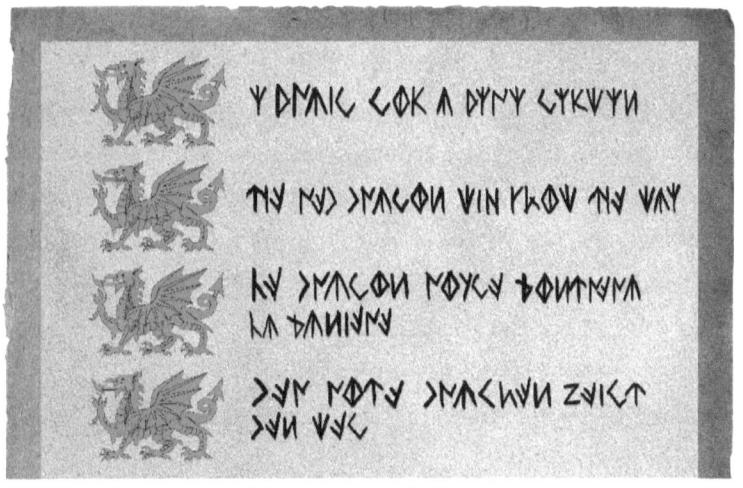

"Freaky." Hamish continued to stare at the page, but nothing else happened. "Now what?"

"Look, the top line is the one line you translated originally that turned out to be Welsh, and when we gave it to Uncle Wynn it translated into English that made sense: THE RED DRAGON WILL SHOW THE WAY. Try the next line."

Hamish did. "Bree, yes, yes, the second line translates directly into English: THE RED DRAGON WILL SHOW THE WAY. It's working." He translated the next two lines. "Oh, bother, it's gone scrambled again."

Briana looked at what Hamish had written, laughed, and pointed at the third line. "No it hasn't. This line is French, the one below it is German."

"You don't speak French or German.

"D'uh. LE DRAGON ROUGE is obviously the Red Dragon, or rather, the dragon red, so it's a good bet the rest is WILL SHOW THE WAY, and that line looks German."

"Oh, yeah. I guess, then, each line is going to say the same thing, in different languages." Hamish browsed through the rest of the book, and tried some further translations. "Nope, it's no good, the other runes are still nonsense."

The two of them sat there staring at the book. Briana turned back to the inside front cover, looked thoughtfully at the runes, and put her forefinger on the little red dragon symbol on the left of the second line of runes, the line that translated directly into English.

As she did so, the other lines changed until they were all the same as the second line of runes. She closed the book and gazed at the front cover. The two lines of runes there seemed different from before.

Hamish grabbed his pen and paper. "Awesome, Bree, it's working, look at this. It now says WELCOME TO THE ATLAS and THE GATEWAY TO THE WORLD, the same as before, except before the runes translated into Welsh, and now they translate into English."

(Note: visit www.theatlaschronicles.com to see larger versions of the runes, their translations, and photos from Briana and Hamish's travels.)

Hamish began translating the runes on the first page. Occasionally he paused in his translations to write out some new notes on the previous alphabet chart he had drawn up.

"What are those?" Briana asked.

"Oh, some English double characters seem to have only one runic character, or are phonetic. It uses *cw* for the English *qu*, and the rune for *ch*, which was used as *ch* in the Welsh words, is also used for the English hard *k*, while the English *ch* is written using the rune for *c* and the rune for *h* rather than the rune for *ch*, and a Z for *z*, which is not on the postcard."

Briana blinked.

Hamish grinned, and continued, "The letter *x* is written as *cs*, so elixir, see here, is written as e-l-i-c-s-i-r. The same rune is used for the Welsh and the English *f*, while the rune used for the Welsh double *ff* is also used for the English *v*, even though a Welsh double *ff* is pronounced as *f*, and a Welsh single *f* is pronounced as *v*. See." He handed her the chart.

⟨ᚡ = cw = English 'qu'
ᚴ = Welsh 'ch' or
      English 'k'
⟨ᚱ = cs = English 'x'
⟨ = 'g' and English 'j'
ᛈ = Welsh and English 'f'
ᚠ = Welsh 'ff' or
      English 'v'

Briana glanced at it. "Like I said, I'll take your word for it."

Hamish continued to translate the rest of the runes on the

page, and read it out to Briana when he'd finished.

"So, according to what's written here we can use this book to live forever, or rule the world, or have lots of money, or whatever? An elixir that gives immortality? What, something like the Philosopher's Stone? That's impossible."

Hamish smiled. "Well, Nicholas Flamel, the inventor of the Philosopher's Stone, was a real person."

"No, he was a character written by J. K. Rowling."

Hamish shook his head. "No. I mean, granted, the Flamel in Potter is a fictional version of the man, as is the Nicholas Flamel in *The Immortal Secrets* series, but both were based on a real person, the real Nicholas Flamel. He lived from 1330 to 1418 and developed a posthumous reputation as an alchemist for his actual work on the Philosopher's Stone.

Briana scoffed. "You're having me on."

"No, it's all true. In 1378 a sage he met in Spain told him a book Flamel owned was a copy of the original *Book of Abramelin the Mage*. Flamel made it his life's work to understand the text of that book. He and his wife decoded enough of the book to recreate its recipe for the Philosopher's Stone. They managed to produce both silver and gold."

"You're making that up."

"No, honestly, I read it on Wikipedia."

"Oh, well then, it must be true. Hamish, anyone can write anything on Wikipedia. It's hardly academically reliable."

"Maybe not, but I've also read about him in real encyclopaedias, printed paper ones. And J. K. Rowling and Michael Scott aren't the only ones who have alluded to him, you know. He was mentioned in The Da Vinci Code, and in the novel *Indiana Jones and the Philosopher's Stone*. In the DC

Comics universe the character Zatanna is said to be a direct descendant of Flamel's. Remember, fiction is often based on fact. Now, let's see what the second page of the introduction says."

When he had finished he read his translation out to Briana.

"You really have to be kidding now. What, we answer some riddles, and talk to a book, and then it's going to magically take us to a place where we need to collect an ingredient for a magic potion off a monster who is waiting to kill us?"

"Yeah, baby."

"Hamish, this is mad."

"It's brilliant."

"It's scientifically impossible."

"Maybe not. I know it sounds crazy, Bree, but this book could do what it says it can. How else do you explain the key and the moving writing and the green and purple smoke and the medieval knight and that Alasdair Toddington of yours? If you believe in all that, why can't you believe in this too?"

"Because, as I just said, it's scientifically impossible."

"Really? If you went back in time to, say, the middle ages, with a cell phone, a laptop, and a microwave oven, wouldn't they say those were scientifically impossible?"

Briana could see Hamish's wide point, but still argued the specifics of it. "Yes, but there's a difference between a cell phone and a book that operates using magic and mythology."

"Maybe it's just different technology."

"I still say it's impossible."

Hamish turned a page. "What the? Where'd the map go?"

The book was still showing runes on the left-hand page, but instead of the map on the right-hand page there was now a giant question mark. As Hamish turned another page, and quickly flicked through the rest of the book, Briana saw no other pages any longer had runes, maps, or question marks.

"What happened?" she asked. "Where did everything go?"

"No idea," Hamish replied, before turning back to the one page still displaying runes. He started to translate them.

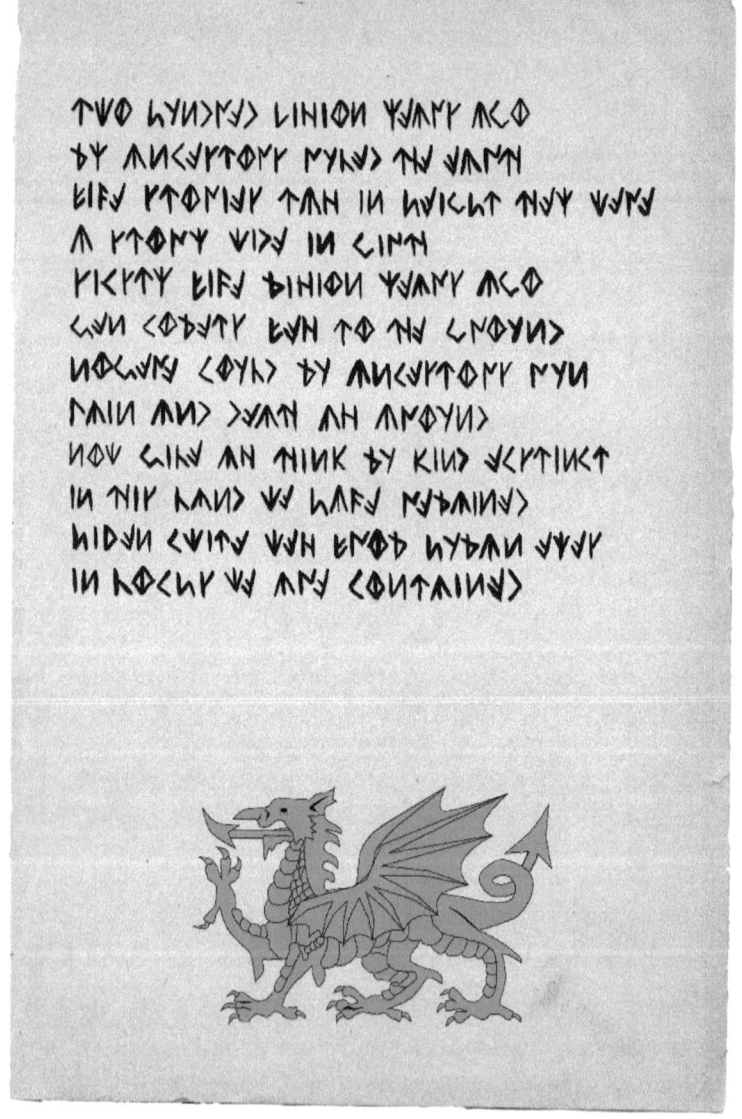

After he had translated these runes he again read the result to Briana.

"No way. That refers to the period the dinosaurs lived. You cannot tell me this book is going to take us back to the time the dinosaurs lived. Look, no one loves dinosaurs more than I do, but this is a book, Hamish, a book, it's not a transportation device, or a time machine, and time travel is impossible anyway."

"You're the one who's always telling me books are printed time machines."

"Not literally, you idiot. Okay, yes, I've said a historical novel can give people an idea of what it was like to live in the past, and a book can bring the past alive for people who live decades or hundreds of years, or even thousands of years afterward. But they don't really take you back in time."

"Maybe this one does," Hamish argued. "Maybe it takes things one step further. But look, getting back to the riddle, I don't think it's talking about dinosaurs. I mean, yes, in the first part it's talking about them, but the dinosaurs were 'ancestors'. Now, if you combine that with this here," he pointed to the runes which translated to 'lochs', "I'd say this means the Loch Ness Monster. There are people who believe the Loch Ness Monster is descended from the dinosaurs."

"Hamish, while I'll concede Nicolas Flamel may have once been a real person, the Loch Ness Monster does not exist."

Her brother ignored her, speaking instead to himself. "Okay, now, what did it say? Hold the red dragon, tell him the answer."

Hamish touched the red dragon symbol underneath the runes on the left-hand page. "The Loch Ness Monster."

The question mark on the right-hand page disappeared, and was replaced by a faint map that gradually increased in colour. When Hamish took his finger off the red dragon, the map stopped. He touched the red dragon again and the map filled in until it clearly showed a map of Scotland. When nothing else happened, Hamish took his finger off the red dragon.

The symbol moved from the left-hand page to the right-hand page, toward the northern end of what Briana presumed was Loch Ness, the western shore. As Briana watched, Hamish again touched the red dragon with one finger. As he did so, blue smoke issued from the book, similar to the green and purple smoke Briana had seen around Alasdair and the mysterious knight.

The smoke flowed over Hamish, snugly forming a cocoon around his body. When he held his hands out, the smoke moved with him, and as Briana watched, his hands dissolved into the smoke.

"Hamish," Briana cried, a note of panic creeping into her voice, as she reached out for him. As her hands entered the smoke, she too was cocooned by it and began to dissolve, as did Rashid, who was still on her lap. Her heart thumped loudly in her ears as she broke out in a cold sweat.

The bedroom disappeared, and Briana found herself moving through a long tunnel of blue stars, although that was more a sensation than an actuality as her body had disappeared completely, and she was now merely a consciousness.

She seemed to gather speed, as the stars raced past faster and faster, until she was flying through a tunnel of streaks of blue light. Terrified and confused, she started to chant, "One, two, three, wake up . . ." when, with a loud 'phpht' the tunnel spat her out. Landing hard on a stone floor (her body had reformed), she heard another 'phpht' as Rashid was spat out next to her. Hamish was already there.

"Wow, this is definitely way, way, waaaay past the far end of weird. Fantastic. Brilliant. Amazing. My God, Bree, do you think we've . . . Bree? Hey, Bree, are you okay?" Hamish took hold of her shoulders and shook her.

Briana stared straight ahead as the blood drained from her face. She slowly raised an arm and pointed a shaking finger toward Rashid, who was scampering up a four-poster bed. At the top he turned, rushed back down, ran over to Briana, and jumped on her lap. "Hey, Mum, I'm really, really, really hungry, do you have anything to eat? I'm famished."

Briana fainted.

VI: Living History

Briana opened her eyes to find Hamish had picked her up and laid her on the bed. He was standing on it, staring out a small window set into the wall above the headboard, while Rashid was swinging off a crossbar of the posts.

"Muuuum, you're awake, do you have any food, I'm huuuungry." He jumped onto the bed. "Mum, I'm really hungry, you know, I'm not, like, just a little bit hungry, but I'm really hungry, do you have any food? Anything at all, I don't mind what it is, I mean, I'd prefer some fruit of course, or some nuts, or maybe some little insects if you happen to have any on you, but really, anything at all would do right now, well, that is, when I say 'anything' I'm really hoping for a lot of 'anything' rather than a little of 'anything', but whatever you have I'll make do with – I'm hungry, Mum."

Hamish looked at her oddly. "Mum?"

Briana replied, "Well, I always thought of him as my baby but I … well … he can't … he isn't … this isn't … ooooooh, this is just totally impossible. My head hurts."

"Muuuuum."

"Sorry, Rashid, I don't have any food." Looking around the small room they were in, Briana saw it was sparsely furnished. Aside from the bed she was on, with a deep red bedspread and matching curtains, the only other items in the room were a wooden chest, two plain wooden chairs, and two small wooden footstools. There were no paintings on the walls, nor decorations or ornaments of any kind. A fireplace was built into the wall opposite the bed and, like the rest of the room, was built of stone.

Hamish grinned at her. "Man, this isn't just pretty close to the far end of weird, this is way, way, waaaay beyond the far end of weird. In fact, this is so far beyond the far end of weird, nothing will ever seem weird again. Bree, this is the coolest, most greatest thing that has ever happened to me. Us. This is fantastic! We," he paused for dramatic effect, "are in a castle on the banks of Loch Ness."

"WHAT?"

Hamish grinned again and jumped onto the floor. "Loch Ness, Bree, we're at Loch Ness. I said 'Loch Ness', well, okay, I said 'Loch Ness Monster', and that book has somehow brought us here. Oh yeah."

"Hamish, that's impossible."

Hamish chuckled, and threw a meaningful look at Rashid. "And he's not? Impossible, I mean." He looked out the window. "Believe what you want, Bree, but we sure as hell ain't in Abergavenny anymore. Take a look for yourself."

Briana stood on the bed and looked out the window, staring at the expanse of water. Her legs shook and she had to sit again.

Hamish patted his pyjamas. "Oh damn, I don't have my phone, I would love to get a photo of this." He walked over to the wooden chest and opened it. "Let's see what's in here. Oh, clothes. Boring. Oh, hang on, maybe not."

After looking through the chest he held up a deep green velvet cloak with gold brocade, an embroidered vest, a doublet, and some funny-looking bubble shorts. "They look medieval."

An impossible thought dawned on Briana, and obviously occurred to Hamish at the same time, as he laughed and jumped up and down on the spot, "Yes, yes, YES. We've travelled back in time, we've travelled back in time, we've travelled back in time, oh yeah. Oh, of course, that's why the tunnel of stars was blue."

"Why?"

"Blue means you've travelled backward in time, red means you've travelled forward in time."

"Where'd you get that from, *Doctor Who*?"

"Well, yes, but it's backed by sound scientific principles as well." He paused. "I think."

"You think?"

"I googled it once and landed on a scientific website talking about blue for backward and red for forward, something to do with the way light travels, but it cost eighteen bucks American to download the article so I didn't bother."

"Time travel is impossible." Briana stubbornly contradicted the growing evidence around her.

"Bree, some of your favourite scientists, such as Stephen Hawking, believe time travel is possible. You should be thrilled that they've been proved correct. You say time travel is impossible? Bree, we've travelled through a book from Abergavenny to Loch Ness, how impossible is that? Rashid is alive, how impossible is that? So, if the book can take us from Wales to Scotland, and can turn Rashid from a stuffed toy into a real living, breathing, and even talking monkey, why can't it take us from one time to another as well? Besides, it was the middle of the night when we left Abergavenny." He pointed out the window. "It is daylight out there now."

The blood, which had slowly returned to Briana's face, drained from it again.

Rashid jumped into Briana's arms, startling her.

"Someone's coming, I can hear footsteps, someone's on their way, maybe they'll come into this room. Hey, maybe they have some food, do you think they have any food, we could ask them, couldn't we?"

Hamish bundled up the clothes he'd taken out, stuffed them back in the chest, closed the lid, grabbed Rashid, and crawled under the bed, firmly putting his hand over the mouth of the chattering monkey.

"Shush, Rashid, quick Bree, get under here. Let's find out who they are first before they catch us trespassing. People in medieval times weren't known for being overly friendly towards strangers."

Briana joined them under the bed just before the door opened with a crash. There was the sound of footsteps, and several pairs of feet came into view.

"Aye," a deep voice with a heavy Scottish accent declared, "this chamburr be suitable fo' ma entertainments. You there, see this room is fit fo' occupation this evening. Scrub the floors, straighten the bed, light a fire and ..."

He stopped as an agonised scream came from outside the window, followed by two more, the last one fading into silence. The bed shuddered above the twins as someone jumped on it and the same voice bellowed out the window, "Trouble, lads?"

A voice came from outside. "No, my Lord, just one of the castle's soldiers we flushed out of hiding from the storage cellar. We'll take the body and throw it with the others."

Briana put her hands over her mouth as she realised she'd just heard a man being killed, and Rashid stopped trying to remove Hamish's hand from his mouth.

The man at the window yelled out of it again. "I wan' this castle checked from one end to the other. I don' wan' any o' Grant's supporters left alive to murder us in oor beds. Search it again, kill any men you find, and send any women and children tae join the others in the Great Hall." He paused.

"Unless you find any particularly fine-looking women, o' course. You can bring them straight to my private chamber where it shall be thair privilege to enjoy the attentions of Sir Donald MacDonald o' Lochalsh fo' the night."

There was laughter from below, and a chorus of, "Aye, Sir Donald."

The bed shuddered as the man jumped off it. "Go and get some firewood and get this room warmed up; it's freezin' in here. I'll be on the castle walls." There was the sound of footsteps leaving and the door shutting.

Briana let out her breath, hardly aware she'd been holding it. "Hamish, they killed someone, and they're coming back and are going to kill any strangers they find," she whispered. "We have to get out of here." She scrambled out from under the bed, followed by Hamish and Rashid, who drew in a breath to say something. "Shush, Rashid, not now." The monkey was more talkative than she'd imagined him to be in the conversations she'd 'had' with him before he came alive, when both sides of the dialogue came from her imagination.

Hamish opened the door a crack and looked out. "Okay, it's all clear, let's go." He paused. "Oh, hang on, we don't want to go out there in our pyjamas, do we?" The twins were still dressed as they had been when they'd left Abergavenny.

Hamish dug through the wooden chest and pulled out two identical dark brown medieval cloaks made of thick wool. Unfortunately there was nothing for their feet, which was a shame as the stone floor was freezing. Knowing the men could be back at any time they put on the cloaks, Briana picked Rashid up, and the three of them left the room and started down the nearest staircase.

Briana suggested they try to find the cellar where the soldiers found the man they had killed. "If they've already searched there, hopefully they won't go back. We could hide there while we decide what to do next."

"Good thinking." Hamish led the way down two levels to where the stairs ended. Cautiously he opened the cellar door a crack, and listened. The twins couldn't hear anything, so they slipped inside. As the door closed behind them, the room plunged into darkness. Briana hastily pushed the door open again so a little bit of light came in. She started running her hands along the wall by the door.

"What are you doing?" Hamish asked.

"Looking for the light switch."

Hamish laughed. "Bree, we're most likely in the Middle

Ages. There won't be a light switch."

"Oh, right." Briana was glad of the dark so Hamish couldn't see her blush.

As her eyes adjusted to the dark, she could dimly make out some of the shapes in the cellar: big round barrels, sacks, earthenware containers, and suchlike. She guessed that the barrels were wine, and the sacks were flour or grain. Rashid scampered over to look for something to eat, and the exclamations of delight that soon drifted back to Briana indicated his search had been successful.

She was thinking of joining him when she heard a noise that sounded like 'phpht phpht' coming from near Rashid.

"Who's there?" Hamish asked, as Briana's heart thumped loudly in her ears.

"Help," came a voice from under one of the sacks, and from under another, "Och, ye regolithic idiot, yer riffling is as great as ever."

The twins went over and cautiously lifted a sack of flour.

"Alasdair," Briana cried in relief, helping him out from under the huge sack, while Hamish helped a second creature out from under another. They were both covered in flour. The newcomer was about Alasdair's height, with a squat little face, and although he was ugly, he had happy, shining eyes and a huge grin, making him cute, in a British bulldog kind of a way.

He was stout and wore black breeches, a white shirt, a red apron, black shoes with huge silver buckles, and a red cap. He stood, dusted himself off, and shook the flour out of his hair.

"Five hunner bloody years, or mair, and ye still cannae riffle properly."

Ignoring him Alasdair fussed around on the floor until he found his pipe, buried in flour, which he dusted off, lit up, and inhaled from deeply, before retrieving his staff from under a sack.

Hamish recognised the name. "Alasdair. So, you're the one Briana was talking about. Wow, you were telling the truth, Bree. Sorry I didn't believe you."

She gave him a tired smile. "That's okay, I didn't believe myself either." Hamish laughed. She turned to face Alasdair and the newcomer. "What are you doing here?"

Alasdair ignored the question. "Lady Briana, Lord Hamish, and Master Rashid, may I introduce my old friend Glynian Kilkenny, the Head Cluricaun of Urquhart Castle."

"Old?" Glynian laughed. "Thair's the pot calling the kettle black."

"The Head what?" Briana asked.

"Cluricaun, he's a cellar spirit, and a cousin to the leprechauns. Mostly they inhabit inns, but my friend Glynian here has a preference for castles."

The cluricaun bowed deeply to Briana and Hamish. "'Tis a pleasure indeed tae mak' yer acquaintance."

"Cousin to the leprechauns, you say?" Hamish asked.

"Aye, laddie."

"That's an awfully thick Scottish accent you have there for an Irishman."

Glynian laughed. "Ma family moved here mony years ago fae Kilkenny, so although Irish in origin, I was born here in Scotland, as was ma faither, Glyn, and ma grandfaither, Ian."

"That would explain it," Hamish commented with a smile. "So," he continued, taking the appearance of the two nonhumans in his stride, "what does a cellar spirit do? A, sorry, what did you say you are?"

"A cluricaun, laddie. A lot of us live in inns in the cellars. As Alasdair explained, I'm partial tae castles masel'. In an inn, if it's well run, we help oot where we can. If it's poorly run, or the owner is cruel tae his staff, we cause havoc: spoil the ale, burst the pipes, let the rats intae the food stores, that sort o' thing."

He chuckled. "Maist humans dinnae even ken we're there. We tak' food and lodgin's, o' course, but ne'er enough so as they knows whit's missin'. An' as tae the havoc we cause or the help we gie, the humans usually attribute their fortunes tae gid luck or bad luck. They dinnae ken it's their ain actions that bring aboot whit they call 'luck'."

Briana was struggling with Glynian's accent, and was about to ask him to clarify a couple of things when she was distracted by Rashid jumping into her arms. Hamish spoke instead, addressing Glynian.

"Did I hear you address Alasdair earlier as a 'regolithic idiot'?"

"Aye, laddie, it's nae very polite but it does best sum him up sometimes." He smiled at the gnome.

Hamish raised an eyebrow. "And is not your use of that particular term in applying it to a person rather than geology somewhat plagiarised? And what's more, plagiarised from an author who lives hundreds of years in your future?"

Glynian laughed. "Well spotted, laddie. Alasdair has supplied me with many fine books from yer time. And if you recognised the term 'regolithic idiot' it's a good bet that you and I are going tae get on just fine." He held out his hand.

"Indeed," Hamish agreed, shaking Glynian's hand.

"Tell me, laddie, I've been dying tae discuss this with someone for years now, ever since I met Alasdair at the end of last century and he gave me some books fae your time. Wha' gender d'ya think Pol . . ."

Alasdair interrupted him. "Not now, Glynian."

"If it's not a rude question, do you mind me asking what you are?" Briana asked Alasdair. "Are you a dwarf?"

He sounded offended. "Goodness, no, I am a gnome."

"A gnome? You don't look much like a gnome," Hamish replied, looking him up and down.

"Well, I'm not your common garden variety."

Hamish laughed.

"Alasdair?" Briana asked in a quiet voice.

"Yes, My Lady."

"What's the date? Now, I mean, you know, here."

"It is the first of November, in the year 1513, My Lady.

VII: Advanced Technology

Briana sat down. After a few moments she broke the silence. "1513? So it's true? We really have travelled back in time? But, but … we can't have, that's impossible. It must be a trick of some kind."

"Bree's a little, ah, stubborn about accepting the impossible, even when it smacks her in the face," Hamish stated with a grin at the other two.

Briana looked up at them. "Of course I'm still struggling to accept. . ." she paused, and sighed in relief. "Dreaming, I'm dreaming. I was on my bed, and we were looking at that book, and I must have fallen asleep, and this is all a . . . ow. Bloody hell Hamish!"

Her brother had pinched her, hard. "Sorry, Bree, it's not a dream, welcome to your new reality. So, Alasdair, 1513, yeah? And we're, what, in Urquhart Castle on the banks of Loch Ness, is that right?"

"Yes, Lord Hamish. I must say, however, that you've picked a terrible time to come and take the Elixir Ingredient from the monster. Sir Donald MacDonald of Lochalsh has invaded the castle. He killed the Laird of the Castle, John Grant of Freuchie, and all the men, and now he holds the women and children captive."

Briana got to her feet again, hoping her legs would hold her. "We didn't choose it on purpose."

"No, I didn't mean that you picked the time consciously," Alasdair apologised. "I meant it's a terrible time to be here. The Atlas takes you to the times where the Elixir Ingredients are, and is not concerned with current local happenings or politics. As the Ingredients have been hidden in different places, so, too, they have been hidden in different times."

"So, you mean it's all true? All that stuff in the Atlas that Hamish translated about the Elixir and what it can do?" Briana asked.

"Yes, My Lady."

"And a book has made us travel through time to a different place, and made Rashid real?"

"Yes, Lady Briana."

Briana looked so pale that Glynian gave her a comforting pat on the back. The gesture was lost as Briana was distracted at that moment by another impossible occurrence as Alasdair clasped his necklace, pointed at the walls, and said "*Light.*"

A line of blazing torches appeared in brackets along the wall. "Can you close the door, Hamish? Thanks. I know the two of you are confused about what's happening."

"You have that right," Briana interrupted, staring at the torches. "How did you . . ."

Alasdair interrupted her interruption, "I'm going to tell you a little bit about what's happening. I hadn't expected to have to do this yet but I need to tell you some things, although not everything. If I told you everything at once you'd go all to pieces on me. I need to ease you into it."

Hamish didn't agree. "What d'ya mean, go to pieces? No way, I'm loving this - tell us everything."

"I wasn't referring to you, Lord Hamish."

"Dude, you can tell *me* everything. Briana, block your ears, or leave the room."

Alasdair sat on one of the sacks, and indicated that the others should join him. "All in good time, My Lord. For now I will tell you that the Questor you read about in the Atlas is someone who embarks on a Quest laid out for them by the Atlas. I was previously a Questor, and currently Lady Briana is a Questor."

"Why her? Why can't I be the Questor? She doesn't believe in this stuff, I do, that's not fair, it should be me, it should be ..."

Alasdair held up his hand. "The first-born. Sorry Lord Hamish, but Lady Briana is the older twin."

"Only by forty-two minutes."

"She is still the firstborn."

"That sucks."

"That is the way it is, My Lord. The Atlas gives the Questor enormous powers and abilities, as long as they have it with them. Lady Briana and I both have the power of the Atlas with us because the Atlas is with us both." He pulled his necklace out from under his shirt and showed it to the twins. Briana had seen him grasp this necklace before, but had never been close enough to observe it properly. Now she could see that it was a tiny gold replica of the book that was currently lying on her bed in Abergavenny.

Briana was stroking Rashid on her lap. "But I don't have," she began, then stopped as she found a necklace, identical to Alasdair's, suspended on a gold chain around her neck. "Oh my goodness, how did that get there?" she asked.

"It appeared there when you answered the first riddle. The Atlas will always be with you now. Even when the Quest is over, and you have passed the Atlas on, your necklace will remain with you."

"Wait a minute, Briana didn't answer the riddle, I did, so that necklace should be mine."

Alasdair's eyes widened. "You answered the riddle? Are you sure?"

"Yes, me, I answered it, and started to dissolve into blue smoke. It was only when Bree grabbed me that she started to dissolve as well, and we ended up here."

"But you couldn't have … unless … well, if that's so … but … I guess, it could have … oh, yes! This is brilliant, BRILLIANT! Glynian, do you know what this means?"

Glynian's grin caused Alasdair to embrace him, and the two of them slapped each other on the back.

Briana glared at the celebratory pair. "If you don't mind, would you care to share the good news?

Alasdair disengaged himself from Glynian's hug, "Oh, Lady Briana, my apologies, but this is such exciting news."

"What is?"

"Umm, ahh, I don't think I should tell you right now."

Briana could feel her temper rising. "Why not?"

"Lady Briana, I'm sorry but . . ."

"And why do you keep calling me *Lady* Briana? And him

Lord Hamish?"

"Ah, well, that's something else I won't tell you yet."

Briana was becoming increasingly frustrated with the gnome. "Is there anything you will tell us yet? You said the necklace gives me enormous powers and abilities. What kind of powers? Is it a magic necklace?"

"No. Well, yes, sort of. Well, not exactly. What I mean is, it's more that it creates a link between you and advanced technology, rather than that it's magic."

"Huh?"

"You know what a USB flash drive is?" he asked her.

"Of course, I'm not stupid."

Alasdair let that slide. "How many photos can you store on one?"

"That depends on the size of the drive and the photos."

"Yes, but size aside, it's safe to say you could store thousands of photos on one, or several hours of video?"

Briana nodded.

Alasdair held up his thumb and forefinger, about three centimetres apart. "And is it not magic that makes it possible to store thousands of photographs, and even hours of movies, on a little piece of metal and plastic this big?"

"No," Briana argued, "it's not magic, it's technology."

Alasdair beamed at her. "Exactly."

Briana looked confused.

"Have you ever seen an old TV show called *The Hitch-Hiker's Guide to the Galaxy*?" Alasdair asked Briana. "Or the movie they made in 2005?"

Briana shook her head.

"Bree is a little behind the eight ball when it comes to sci-fi," Hamish informed him.

"Yes, I know, I've spent years worrying about that. Anyway, long before you were born there was a TV show based on the book of the same name. When it first came out the idea of an electronic storage unit about the size of a Gideon's Bible that contained that much information electronically was pure science fiction. Now, something this size," he held up his thumb and forefinger again, "can store an amount of information that Douglas couldn't have imagined even in his wildest dreams."

"Who's Douglas?" Briana asked.

Hamish rolled his eyes and spoke to Glynian. "I told you she's totally fantasilliterate."

"Fantasilliterate? I like that." The two of them laughed.

Briana glared at them, and Alasdair continued talking.

"When *Star Trek* first aired on TV no one ever dreamed that the video comlinks the crew used to communicate with each other would ever become a reality. Now video cell phones are common. Many things that used to be viewed as magic have become possible through technology.

"Flying for humans was viewed as magic, until the Wright Brothers did it using technology in 1903. Light other than from a fire or candle was thought to be magic, until Thomas Edison improved projects of Humphry Davy and Frederick de Moleyns and patented the light bulb. That's all those kinds of 'magic' are, advanced technology."

Hamish looked thoughtful. "That makes sense. It's like, when Martha said to the Doctor in *The Shakespeare Code* there's no such thing as magic, and what we think of as 'magic' is a different sort of science. Is this the same idea?"

"Hamish, I'm having enough trouble dealing with the impossibilities that are happening around us right now. Can we please leave storylines from sci-fi shows out of it?" Briana implored.

"No, really, I think Gareth Roberts was on the right track."

"Who?"

"A scriptwriter for *Doctor Who*. He said, well the Doctor said, but Roberts wrote the script so it was his words really, he said that humans chose mathematics as a science, and that by using the right sum of numbers and the right equation we can do stuff like split the atom. The Carrionites, they were the aliens in that episode, used words instead and so could do different stuff, which the humans saw as being magic."

He stopped, and turned to face Alasdair. "He was right, wasn't he? If we knew the right words to use, the same way we use the right numbers to split the atom, then who knows what we could do? We'd be able to do stuff that we would call 'magic', wouldn't we? That's how the Atlas works, isn't it? Using words instead of numbers?"

Alasdair considered Hamish's theory, "Kind of, sort of, but not really. It's complicated."

"Simplify it."

Alasdair laughed. "I don't even fully understand it myself."

"Well you could at least tell us where it came from."

"I will tell you when the time is right, but not now."

Hamish persisted. "Why not? Because it'll freak Bree out too much? Briana, like I said earlier, block your ears."

Alasdair laughed. "No, it's not that, we just don't have the luxury of time right now."

"Why not?"

"We just don't."

Hamish continued pleading, but Alasdair wouldn't say anything else.

"Fine," Hamish gave in finally, looked at the wall and waved a hand toward the torches. "Bree has one of those necklaces now. Are you saying that she can do that?"

"Yes, My Lord."

"Well, go on Bree, have a go."

Briana looked at Alasdair. "What do I have to do?"

"Clasp your necklace, picture clearly in your mind what you want to create, and say its name."

"That's it?"

"Basically, although it will take you many attempts before you achieve your first success."

Briana waved one hand vaguely at the wall. "Torch." As she expected, nothing happened.

"Your pardon, My Lady, but you have to mean it. The Atlas will not answer wishy-washy requests."

Hamish laughed. Briana glared at him. She gently removed Rashid from her lap, and stood up. She pointed imperiously at the wall and shouted, *"TORCH."*

An entire row of blazing torches appeared in brackets along the wall above Alasdair's torches, accompanied by a cloud of black smoke. Alasdair's eyes widened at this spectacular success. He hadn't expected that.

Hamish looked stunned. "Fantastic, Bree, that so cool. Can I borrow the necklace and have a go?" He held his hand out.

"My Lord, the Lady Briana will not be able to do that."

"Why not?"

"Well, the necklace won't come off. It won't fit over her head, there is no clasp, and the chain will not break."

Hamish looked impressed. "Like Ce'Nedra's? Cool."

Briana tugged at the necklace, hoping to break the thin chain.

"Ah, Bree, I don't imagine that will work for you any better than it did for Ce'Nedra. You'll cut your skin like she did and it won't come off," Hamish told her.

"Who?" Briana snapped, still tugging at the chain.

Hamish rolled his eyes. "Never mind."

"Never mind? NEVER MIND? What do you mean, *never mind?*" She pointed an accusing finger at Alasdair. "He has chained this thing about my neck and tells me it will be there for the rest of my life, and you tell me 'never mind'. I bloody well do mind."

"The lassie may no' have heard of Ce'Nedra, but her reaction is the same," Glynian observed seriously to Hamish. Hamish laughed, and Glynian joined in.

"Shut up, you two, this is not funny."

Hamish and Glynian laughed even harder.

"You don't have to shout," Alasdair told Briana.

"I think I'm entitled to shout a bit, don't you?"

"My apologies, I didn't mean you don't have to shout at – will you two stop it – I didn't mean don't shout at them. I meant when you harness the power of the necklace you don't have to shout; you just have to be serious about doing what you want to do."

"Do or do not, there is no try," Hamish said, bringing another laugh forth from Glynian.

"I'm having a little trouble adjusting to all of this, and you two laughing at me doesn't help." She glared at Hamish and Glynian.

The cluricaun looked a little embarrassed, but Hamish returned her look calmly, with a smirk on his lips. Then he spoke to Glynian. "Dude, I'm famished. Let's go see if there's anything to eat back there." The two of them headed toward the back of the cellar, followed by Rashid who was ready for seconds.

Alasdair sat quietly with Briana, not speaking. He didn't think she was ready to hear the whole truth yet, especially about where the Atlas was from, and the secret about her own ancestry.

He knew that Briana was aware of the part of her ancestry that stretched back through Owain Glyndŵr over a thousand years to the Princes of Powys and Deheubarth, but that was only half the story. If he was to tell her of the other half of her ancestry while she was in this state, that startling revelation could possibly send her over the edge.

VIII: Keeper of the Atlas

B riana roused herself and was about to ask Alasdair some more about the Atlas, despite not really wanting to hear the answers, when Hamish beat her to it. He called out from the back of the cellar while he chewed on a mouthful of bread and cheese he'd found. "Alasdair, where did you get the Atlas from and what's your connection to it? Are you its keeper?"

"That's exactly what I am, Keeper of the Atlas. I have been looking after it for a long time now."

"And how did you come to be that?"

Alasdair paused a moment before answering. "Through circumstance, really. When I first, ah, found the Atlas, it was only chance that I, and not someone else, found it. However, as events surrounding it unfurled, and I completed my Quest, passed it on, and then became aware of its true history and purpose, I took it upon myself to retrieve it and become its Keeper until such time as it needed to be passed on again."

"To Briana. Why her? There's nothing special about her?"

"Thanks," Briana retorted.

Alasdair smiled. "Actually, you are both special, and I will tell you everything you want to know eventually, but not yet."

"Why not?" Hamish asked.

Alasdair looked uncomfortable. "I'll tell you what you need to know as you need to know it. I don't want you worrying about what is to come before you need to."

"You're kidding?" Hamish replied. "That's intended to make us not worry? That's like a doctor saying 'don't worry, this won't hurt a bit' before sticking a dirty great needle in your arm. Seriously, tell us everything now," he demanded.

"I know you're impatient, Hamish, but I have been Keeper of the Atlas for a long time, and I don't want to do anything or say anything that would put in jeopardy what I have protected for so long."

"How long?" Briana asked.

"Well, I was born in 1444 at Raglan Castle in . . ."

Hamish interrupted the gnome. "Bree said she met you in our time, so does that mean you travelled forward to our time from yours? You're from our past?"

"You'll find out if you stop interrupting me."

"Oh, sorry."

"Raglan Castle is about ten miles southeast of Abergavenny, where you two are currently in your own time."

This time Briana interrupted. "What do you mean where we are 'currently in our own time'? You mean there's a Briana and Hamish back where we were? Or, I guess, if we're in the past now, they're in the future. I mean, oh, umm, I don't even know what I mean. Are we here, or there?"

"Both and neither," Alasdair replied. Briana frowned.

"You're here, but you're not, and you're still there, but you're not." Briana's frown deepened.

"One of your cats is called Schrödinger, yes? Well, since you have a cat called Schrödinger, you must be familiar with the experiment?"

"Yes I am, but it doesn't bear out what you're hinting toward. Schrödinger proposed the experiment to illustrate what he saw as the problems of the Copenhagen Interpretation of quantum mechanics, not to prove there was such a thing as time travel."

Alasdair smiled. "Ah, but the Copenhagen Interpretation was, in fact correct, and there are multiple realities which all exist as a 'probability wave function'. Only when this function collapses does 'reality' occur. You're here, but you're also back in your own time. You're in alternate realities that have not yet collapsed into reality."

"So, we're not in the past, we're in a parallel world?" Briana asked, struggling with the concept.

"No, that's different again. You're in an alternate reality of your world, in the past. I mean, you're in the past of your actual reality, but because in your reality you haven't been to the past, this past is both an alternate reality to your own time, and the same reality with you as an addition. As you move from one time to another you are, in essence, still where you started from too because, since time can be in all places at once, so too can you be in several places at once." He paused to let Briana consider what he'd told her, then carried on. "Furthermore, no matter how long you stay here you'll find that when you go home you'll arrive back at the same time you left. When you move through time to a specific time, once you arrive the time you spend there doesn't affect your time because your time hasn't happened yet, and even if it had, because the realities are different it wouldn't affect your time, anyway."

Briana continued to stare at Alasdair.

"You're not really back in your own time either, because you're here, but you're still sort of there in the sense that no one will notice you're not, although that's more because space and time are different aspects of the same thing in the same way that matter and energy are. Changing location necessitates changing time. Changing time, but remaining in the same location, is not allowed, except in reality, which is observably what happens. Time ticks away at the location we are at."

Briana shook her head, while Hamish laughed from the back of the cellar. "Okay, dude, I so didn't follow any of that, but I don't care how we ended up here, I'm just stoked we are here. Time travel. Man, this rocks." Hamish and Glynian came back to where Alasdair and Briana were sitting. They each dragged a sack of grain behind them, and pummelled them into abstract seats before sitting down.

"So, how did we travel here?" Hamish continued, quickly adding, "And I don't mean more of that techno-babble timey-wimey explanation stuff. I mean, what was it that we travelled through? It didn't look like a *Star Trek* or *Farscape* wormhole, it obviously wasn't the time vortex that the Doctor uses, and although it's a long time since I've read *The Magician* I don't think it was a rift."

"It was a riffle," Alasdair replied.

"What's a riffle?"

"It's similar to the methods you mentioned, but different."

"Different how?"

"It's like a car, bus, and train are different, but still get you from point A to point B."

Hamish grinned. "You mean from century A to century B?"

Alasdair smiled. "Exactly. Anyway, getting back to my story, I was born at Raglan Castle. It's a tourist attraction nowadays, and mostly in ruins but, oh, it was magnificent in its day." His eyes brimmed slightly.

"The beautiful Long Gallery with its timber panelling was gorgeous, and its windows, which overlooked the lovely manicured lawns of the Fountain Court, were superb. The walls were lined with portraits of the Earls of Worcester, and there was a great open fireplace with ornate carvings and sculptures, a long hall, decorous state apartments, and an impressive gatehouse. It was a wonderful, superb castle to call home." He stopped, sniffed, and wiped his eyes on his sleeve.

"Reminiscing about what was, does no one any good," he sighed. "My parents were the castle's Head Gnomes, Arthur and Miranda Toddington. The castle was under the Lordship of Sir William ap Thomas, who had previously been the Steward of the Lordship of Abergavenny, the Steward of the Duke of York's estates in Wales, and Sheriff of Cardiganshire, Carmarthenshire, and Glamorgan. He died the year after I was born, and was succeeded by his eldest son William, who took the surname of Herbert. Sir William is buried at St. Mary's in Abergavenny, along with some of your ancestors.

"They were volatile times in those days, and on the second of February in 1461 my father was killed fighting with Sir

William Herbert at the Battle of Mortimer's Cross in Here-fordshire. My mother never recovered from my father's death, and she died a few months later." Alasdair sniffed again, and Briana wiped her own watering eyes. "So, at the age of eighteen, with both my parents dead, I left Raglan Castle to explore Europe.

"I returned in 1469 to the castle, and fought in Sir William Herbert's army at the Battle of Edgecote on July the twenty-sixth, where Sir William and his brother Sir Richard Herbert were both executed. Richard Neville, the Earl of Warwick, gave me permission to accompany the bodies back to Abergavenny for burial at St. Mary's. He was known as the Kingmaker and ultimately came to a sticky end himself after falling out with his protégé, King Edward, the elder brother of Richard III.

"I liked Abergavenny, and settled there for a while, taking a job at Abergavenny Castle looking after the horses. I'm fond of castles, and of churches, and of exploring, and it was a couple of years later, while wandering through parts of the upstairs level of St. Mary's that I, umm, probably shouldn't have been in, that I found the Atlas.

"I gradually discovered how it worked, solved all the riddles, fought monsters, giants, and other creatures, and gathered together all the ingredients for my Elixir."

Hamish interrupted. "So you've already fought the Loch Ness Monster?" Briana could hear the excitement in his tone.

"No, the Atlas changes the riddles for each Questor, so my challenges were different to what yours will be. Once I'd gained all the Ingredients I made the Elixir and, still being only twenty-seven, young and reckless and wanting to live forever, I chose Immortality."

Alasdair looked at the twins in turn. "The young all want to live forever, but let me tell you, it's no fun to live for hundreds of years and have to watch all your family, and most of your friends, grow old and die. I rue the day I made that choice.

"I won't tell you all my adventures now, it would take too long. But I do need to tell you what happened after I'd finished my Quest, and I passed the Atlas on to someone else.

"During my Quest I became good friends with Sir Gawain, King Arthur's nephew, so I decided to pop back in time to 675 and visit him, hoping to get some advice on whom to give the Atlas to."

This time Briana interrupted. "You knew King Arthur? You mean he was a single real person, not a conglomeration of many stories about different people?"

"Oh, he was real all right. A better human I have rarely met, and Lancelot, too, wonderful lads both of them. It was such a tragedy they loved the same woman. Anyway, over a drink with Gawain I happened to mention my love of dragons, and he told me about a man by the name of Cadeyrn Llewellyn, who lived up north, near where the modern-day town of Llanberis in Gwynedd is, in Snowdonia. He said that Cadeyrn had recently built a dragon sanctuary there."

"A dragon sanctuary?" Briana interrupted again. "You mean to say that dragons actually, really, truly existed?"

"Of course. Why do you think they appear in so many of your myths and legends? Because they're based on truth."

"But if dragons existed, why isn't there any evidence left?

Skeletons or something?"

"When a dragon dies, the body is consumed by flame, a bit like a phoenix but, of course, they don't rise from the ashes like phoenixes do. No skeleton, no proof they ever existed, and, of course, they're all extinct now. Anyway, Gawain said he'd heard that this Cadeyrn was crazy about dragons too, same as I was. At that point in time they were an endangered species, and Cadeyrn wanted to dedicate his life to saving them from extinction."

Briana raised one eyebrow. "I hardly think the concept of 'extinction' would have been around in 675."

"Well, no, he wasn't aware of the concept of 'extinction' back then, but he was aware that the numbers of dragons had dropped off severely over the previous decade or so as dragon hunting had become more popular. He wanted to breed them and get their numbers back up, so he started a private sanctuary, called Caelaelia Vasadori, to run a breeding program, or so he told people.

"He had built a large castle on the grounds between 670 and 675, and once he started keeping dragons the place became popular with people coming to visit. When Gawain told me about it I knew what I wanted to do with my life: work for Cadeyrn Llewellyn at Caelaelia Vasadori and dedicate myself to his cause of dragon conservation. I also decided to pass the Atlas on to him. I was sure he could use it for the good of the sanctuary and to improve the life of the dragons living there.

"At this time he had gained a certain amount of fame throughout the surrounding area, and was widely known as the Dragon Lord. Gawain said that he had heard Cadeyrn was a kind man, gently spoken, who spent every waking moment with the dragons, taking care of them and looking after them. I riffled north, introduced myself, and had a long conversation with Cadeyrn.

"I must say, I was a bit taken aback. Caelaelia had such a good name, and yet when I arrived there the place seemed disorganised, and Cadeyrn himself seemed a bit vague about what went on there. But he did seem kind and gentle, and he had been away for several weeks visiting another sanctuary, so I put aside any misgivings I had and started working there. From day one I found myself running the place." He paused. "It was the best two months of my life."

Briana looked surprised. "You only lasted two months? What happened?"

Briana could see the hurt in his eyes. "I went to talk to Cadeyrn one night after I'd finished work, and told him about the Atlas. He'd been away several times during the time I'd been there, so I confess I hadn't really spent that much time with him. But he appeared such a gentle soul I trusted him completely. I knew that the Sanctuary was short of resources and was struggling to feed the dragons and get decent-sized enclosures built. If Cadeyrn went on a Quest he could choose Wealth, and all of Caelaelia's problems would be over. Some of the dragons were in awfully small cages, although, in hindsight, Cadeyrn's own castle was large and comfortable. Of course, he didn't believe me at first, until I riffled him back a few days in time to prove it was possible."

"Wasn't that dangerous?" Hamish asked. "You're not supposed to go back on your own personal timeline."

"I know, but I was careful. It was to prove a point, we

were only there for a few minutes, and I made sure we didn't change anything and our past selves didn't see us. We stayed long enough to convince him, and then went back to our present, where I gave the Atlas to him.

"I have to confess, I did have a few reservations about him, but they were all vague misgivings that were easy to brush aside. There was nothing I could put my finger on, just a feeling that he was, well, a bit odd. But I was swayed by my love of dragons, so I put aside those misgivings, gave him the Atlas, and riffled forward to 1471 to collect my belongings from Raglan, and to prepare to move back to 675 to work full time at Caelaelia. It took me a few weeks to get everything sorted out and to say my good-byes to everyone. I told them I was moving to another village, because I could hardly tell people I was moving to 675, and then headed back to Caelaelia to begin my life's work as a dragon conservationist.

"After I arrived back, Cadeyrn avoided me for several days, which was a bit strange, but during this time I was pretty busy finding somewhere to live and moving in, so I didn't worry too much. However once I finally tracked him down, he was distant and abrupt with me, and told me that he was uncomfortable about the way I moved there hoping he would give me work. He told me I was no longer welcome at Caelaelia, and had me thrown off the property by goblins."

"That doesn't seem fair. Couldn't you do anything?" Briana asked.

"Like what? There was no such thing as a Department of Labour in those days, and besides, everyone believed Cadeyrn's public persona, so he would have gotten away with whatever he wanted to do anyway. I later found out I was only the latest in a long line of people that Cadeyrn had done this to."

"So what did you do?"

"I was so upset that I couldn't stay anywhere near Caelaelia. I couldn't stand being near and not being allowed to enter, so I returned to Raglan Castle in 1471, telling my friends and family I'd gotten homesick in the other village. Over the next few months I would riffle back to Cadeyrn's time every so often, and I heard many bad stories about him.

"For example, I discovered that he hadn't set the sanctuary up himself, as he had claimed. Caelaelia Vasadori was originally built even further north by a husband and wife who ran it with their children under the name of Sheli Tysaelor. Unfortunately the husband was killed in a hunting accident, and his wife and children struggled to keep the sanctuary running. Cadeyrn heard about it and presented himself as the answer to their prayers, told them that he knew all about dragon husbandry, moved in, and gradually took over.

"One day the wife and her children came home from a visit to see her brother, and found everything gone, and I mean everything. Cadeyrn had taken the dragons, all the fencing and enclosures, and had even dismantled the build- ings and packed the building materials, taking everything south, leaving the family with nothing but shattered dreams and no way of getting anything back."

IX: Dragons and Paradoxes

Briana was shocked anyone could do that to someone who was grieving, and was about to say something when Alasdair continued. He told them of his disillusionment with Cadeyrn Llewellyn and the sanctuary.

"I talked to others who had been through what I had, and heard awful stories about how Cadeyrn treated the dragons, and about a breeding program he had started to produce white dragons.

"There were nine species of dragons: Bengal Firebreathers, they're orange; Indochinese Longwings, which are a dark gray; Malayan Shortclaws, which are a kind of dusky brown; Sumatran Acidsprayers, which are your typical mythological green; Siberian Longtooths, which are bronze; the rare Balinese Fastflyers, which are silver; the even rarer Javan Slashclaws, which are gold; the red Caspian Jumpers; and the South China Shortwings, which are yellow and can't fly too well. In the wild . . ."

"Wait a minute," Briana interrupted in a surprised tone.

"Those names sound suspiciously like a list of tiger breeds. You're not going to tell me that dragons didn't become extinct, but instead evolved into tigers, are you?"

Alasdair laughed. "No, no, but you are right, the names of today's tiger breeds were taken from the names of the old dragon breeds."

Hamish raised an eyebrow. "And how, exactly, did that happen?"

"I mentioned a thing or two here and there to certain people at certain times. It was a tragedy that the dragons went extinct, but at least I managed to keep their names alive."

"Except for the Javan, Caspian, and Balinese," Briana said, referring to the three species of extinct tigers.

"Yes, that was a double blow when not only the dragons, but the tigers who kept their names alive, became extinct. Anyway, where was I? Oh yes, white dragons. In the wild, very, very occasionally, a Bengal Firebreather would be born white instead of orange, but they never survived long. They were always sickly because their whiteness was the result of a defective gene, and Mother Nature disposed of them the way she does with the weak and defective, you know, survival of the fittest and all that.

"Cadeyrn and his friends were out hunting dragons one day, when . . ."

Briana was horrified. "Hunting dragons? You said he was a dragon conservationist."

"Well, he was, but rich people paid well for dragon skins and Cadeyrn was never above putting his own needs before those of the dragons. He killed a lot of wild dragons and sold their skins to raise the money he needed to add to his castle and breed captive dragons."

"Strange method of conservation," Hamish observed.

"Strange sort of man. So, yes, they were out hunting one day when the beaters drove a mother dragon into Cadeyrn's path, who he shot and killed with several arrows. As he was congratulating himself four dragonlets wandered into the clearing, and one was white. Seeing the opportunity for great profit, Cadeyrn killed the orange ones and kept the white one.

"When the dragonlet grew up he tried to breed from him, but all the babies came out orange, until he experimented with inbreeding. That resulted in many white dragonlets, but most were stillborn or died shortly after birth from deformities due to inbreeding. Still, he got a few 'good ones' he could keep."

"What sort of deformities?" Briana asked quietly. How could someone do that just to make a profit?

"Immune deficiencies, scoliosis of the spine, cleft palates, mental impairments, and grotesquely crossed eyes that bulged from the skull. Actually, all white dragons are cross-eyed, whether it shows or not, because the gene that makes their skin white also causes the optic nerve to be wired to the wrong side of the brain. That's another reason Cadeyrn is keen to have white dragons: because of their defective eyesight, they are far more dependent upon their masters, and despite his public image, Cadeyrn is not a good dragon tamer.

"You need to work with an animal every day, but Cadeyrn has bred so many dragons that he can't possibly spend that much time with each one. And anyway, he only bothers to spend time with them when he is showing off to visitors. The rest of the time he ignores them. He has two other dragon tamers working at Caelaelia Vasadori, who do all the real work with the dragons. When visitors come, Cadeyrn steps in and takes all the glory."

"What does he do with all the dragonlets?" Briana asked. "The deformed ones, I mean."

"He throws them down a pit and leaves them to die. He takes it as a personal insult when they are born deformed due to his inbreeding practices."

"That's horrible. And you gave this man the Atlas?"

"I didn't find all this out till it was too late, and I've beaten myself up about it so many times since then. Hindsight is a poignantly painful experience."

Alasdair looked so guilty and upset that Briana back-pedalled quickly. "Well, if you didn't find all this out until after you'd given him the Atlas it's not your fault then, is it?"

"I still wish I'd listened to my misgivings though. Anyway, I could go on and on about the stories of the people whose lives he has destroyed, but we'd be here for days. I heard later that he had, of course, gone on his Quest, and again demonstrated his abhorrent way of using others to further his own desires and goals. He gathered together a group of brownies, goblins, pixies, and gremlins, and used them to defeat the monsters, sacrificing many lives in the process rather than undertaking anything dangerous himself."

Hamish nodded. "Cannon fodder."

"Exactly. He was not a brave man, but that all changed after he chose Immortality. He gained a number of powers along the way, which is not good for someone who has no moral sense of the difference between right and wrong."

Hamish frowned. "So where is he now? I mean, if he's

Immortal, he's still alive and, I guess, still running a dragon sanctuary in north Wales. Wouldn't people kind of notice that in our time?"

"He's not there now, and I mean 'now' as in 'your time'. When Llewellyn ap Iorwerth, also known as Llewellyn the Great, built Dolbadarn Castle, south of present-day Llanberis at the tip of Llyn Padarn, in the early 1200s, Cadeyrn took action. He was fiercely protective of his privacy, and believed the construction of Llewellyn the Great's castle would lead to many new people moving to the area."

Hamish chuckled. "A bit confusing with two Llewellyns."

"There weren't that many names to go around in those days," Alasdair explained.

Briana agreed. "Don't I know it. I became so confused when I was putting together our family tree. For hundreds of years our ancestors were pretty much only called William, Richard, or John."

Alasdair laughed. "Yes, humans weren't terribly inventive back then. Anyway, as it turned out Cadeyrn was mistaken about an influx of people; Dolbadarn fell to the English Army in 1283, and two years later the castle was abandoned and its timber used by the English for the construction of nearby Caernarfon Castle. The area was deserted and Llanberis itself wasn't settled until about two hundred years ago as a result of the slate industry, a very young village by Welsh standards. But Cadeyrn wasn't to know that, and in 1250 he decided to move his entire castle and Caelaelia Vasadori back in time to the seventh century, to 655 to be specific, twenty-one years before he drank the Elixir."

Hamish blinked. "That was some undertaking."

"Oh, it was, it was huge. It took him about five years. The entire castle had to be taken apart brick by brick. Cadeyrn riffled the bricks by the barrow load back to 655. The castle was reassembled there, after which the dragon enclosures, and finally the dragons, were riffled back."

Briana was puzzled. "If it took him five years to move the castle back from the thirteenth century, wouldn't he have taken five years to rebuild it in the seventh century? Wouldn't he have finished it in 660?"

"No, My Lady. Cadeyrn used the Atlas to create a time loop that fixed the castle in 655, which is where it still exists today."

"Why didn't he riffle the whole castle back in one go, though? Why take it apart brick by brick?"

"Hamish can answer that."

Hamish looked at the gnome quizzically.

"No doubt you've read *The Belgariad* series and the *Eragon* novels?"

"*Eragon* once. The Eddings books I read every year."

"Well then. what did Belgarath tell Garion about using his powers? What did Brom tell Eragon? The same principle applies to the Atlas."

"Oh, right." Hamish turned to Briana. "It takes as much effort to use the powers of magic, or sorcerery, or, I presume, of the Atlas, as it does to physically do something. If he had tried to take the castle back in one piece using his powers, it would have been like trying to lift and carry it by himself. Correct Alasdair?"

"Correct."

Hamish frowned. "Hang on. If he took the whole castle

back to 655 from 1250, and held it there in a time loop, but the castle already existed in 675, cos you said he built it between 670 and 675, then once he went back to 655, wouldn't that create a paradox when 670 came around because … ahhhh, wait, hang on, I confused myself. What was I asking?"

Alasdair smiled. "Moving back along his own timeline and re-building the castle before he built it the first time did, indeed, create a paradox. However, Cadeyrn managed to circumvent the paradox by riffling forward to 675 and killing his future-self, before his future-self drank the Elixir in 676. This meant that his past-self took the place of his future-self in that time continuum, and everything that his future-self was supposed to have done ceased to exist, and was replaced by his past-self and everything that his past-self had done as his future-self before riffling back to the past."

Briana was struggling to follow the conversation. "But if he killed his future-self, the one who drank the Elixir, wouldn't the past-self, in 655, no longer be Immortal?"

"No, what his future-self had done *became* part of his past-self, even though he had killed his future-self."

Briana blinked, and Hamish laughed. "Okay, dude, way more convoluted than *Continuum*, we'll just take your word for it. So, he lives perpetually in 655?"

"Yes, far enough back in time that no solid historical data about Caelaelia Vasadori exists in your present time, and whatever stories do filter down through the centuries are termed 'mythology' or 'legends' in your time."

"Ain't time travel something, Bree?" Hamish laughed at the look of confusion on Briana's face, before turning back to

Alasdair. "So, you said he chose Immortality, the same as you did?"

"Yes, and then he chose Wealth. Cadeyrn hungers for power, but with unlimited wealth he could buy unlimited power. Money is power, no matter what time you live in."

"But how could he get two Elixirs?" Briana asked, remembering the first translations Hamish had done from the Atlas. *"One Gift, One Choice*, after which you have to pass it on, that's what the Atlas said. He doesn't sound like the sort of man who'd willingly pass it on to someone else."

"Indeed, no, and he was furious when the Atlas wouldn't work for him anymore. So, he passed it on to the head dragon keeper at Caelaelia, Gryffydd Vaughan, who had been friends with Cadeyrn since they were teenagers.

"With the assistance of Cadeyrn, Gryffydd worked through the Atlas and attained all the Ingredients for the Elixir, which Cadeyrn offered to store safely for him in his castle. Once Gryffydd had all the ingredients, he made the Elixir, but as he tipped his head back to drink it, Cadeyrn cut his throat from behind. He drank the Elixir himself and chose Wealth as his old friend Gryffydd lay dying before him."

"And Cadeyrn? Where is he now?" Hamish asked. "I mean, does he stay at his Castle in 655, or does he travel around in time like you do?"

"He travels, although not as much over the last few centuries as he used to. He holds the castle and everyone in it in 655, but is still able to travel to anywhere in time, up to whatever the current time is, as if he was living outside the castle in free-flowing time. He . . ."

Alasdair was cut off by a blinding flash of purple light and an explosion that blasted the door to the cellar apart. Briana screamed, Rashid jumped off her lap with a screech, and Alasdair, Glynian, and Hamish scrambled to their feet.

The medieval knight, who the twins had seen briefly at Dan-yr-Ogof and Tyn-y-Bryn, stood in the doorway and looked around the cellar.

Briana had only seen him from the back at Dan-yr-Ogof, and in their bedroom at Tyn-y-Bryn he had been silhouetted against the windows, so she hadn't seen his face. Now, up close, and in the light from the torches, she could see him clearly.

His short-cropped hair and stubbled beard framed a classically strong jaw line. There was only one word to describe him: gorgeous. Even the faint scar that ran above and below his right eye, and the one on his left cheek, added to his magnetism, rather than detracting from his perfection, giving the knight a compelling attraction.

And that was an unusual reaction for Briana to have. She had no idea what her friends meant when they said this boy was gorgeous, or that boy was ugly, something that astounded her friends. They would show her yearbook photos of boys who, they said, were the ugliest in their school, and show her photos of Hollywood A-listers or pop stars, and demand to know how she could not tell that one group was ugly and the other gorgeous. To Briana, she might as well have been looking at photos of sheep – they all looked the same to her.

It was the same with women. To her, none of her friends looked any different from the women on the cover of magazines although, strangely, she could tell the difference in her own face whether she had make-up on or not. Eventually her friends grudgingly conceded she couldn't see any difference, and decided maybe she was hot-blind, like some people were colour-blind.

It was a shock to Briana to see this man who epitomised everything her friends described their favourite actors and singers as, and she was inexplicably drawn to him.

He turned to look at her, and smiled a half-smile that was almost, but not quite, a smirk. As the knight's piercing eyes met hers, she couldn't tear her eyes away from his, even though a small part of her mind screamed at her to break the connection.

She was spared from maintaining eye contact any longer as the knight turned away from her and focused his attention on Alasdair. "Hello, Toddington," he drawled softly "It's been a long time."

"On the contrary, Cadeyrn, I still remember what you did to me as if it was yesterday.

X: A Flight Across the Loch

Briana's heart pounded in her ears as the knight strode into the room. He stood with hands on hips and laughed. "Oh my dear Alasdair, have you still not gotten over that?" He shook his head, and changed the subject.

"Do they know?"

Alasdair returned his gaze, but stayed silent.

Cadeyrn laughed. "How like you, you haven't told them yet. It's a pity they are going to die without knowing who they are, or who you had hoped they would be. Oh well, so be it. I have other matters to attend to."

Without warning he pointed directly at Briana. "*Fire.*" She heard Alasdair cry out as a blast of purple fire shot toward her. Instinctively, she threw her hands in front of her face in a protective gesture. A cloud of black smoke surrounded her, and the fire rebounded and vanished as though it had hit a force field.

Cadeyrn raised one eyebrow at Alasdair, who had fallen over in his haste to help Briana and had missed seeing what happened. "So," the knight drawled softly, "you have at least revealed some knowledge to them. No matter. I doubt you have had enough time to …"

There was a loud thump, followed by an explosive white cloud and a huge clatter as the knight toppled to the floor. Hamish and Glynian had hit him from behind with a sack of flour, which had burst. "Run!" Alasdair cried, and everyone bolted through the empty door frame.

They ran down a large hall, through a doorway that led outside into a courtyard, and over a little wooden footbridge spanning a deep ditch where they found themselves in the area of the castle where McDonald's men had killed the soldier.

"Now what?" asked Hamish. "If we run out there," he gestured past the castle walls, "the soldiers will get us. If we stay here, Llewellyn will get us. Do something, Briana."

"Like what?" Everything was happening so fast that Briana couldn't think.

"I dunno. Create a flying carpet or something."

Before Briana could do anything, an explosion rumbled through the ground, obviously originating from the storage cellar. Soldiers ran past them and through the doorway heading towards the explosion as the sound of another one, accompanied by cries of pain, rippled through the courtyard. One soldier was thrown backwards out of the doorway and crashed into a wall. Briana didn't know whether he was unconscious or dead.

Cadeyrn Llewellyn strode through the doorway, purple smoke billowing around him. The soldiers lined up in front of him and started shooting arrows. He retaliated with small balls of purple fire that shot from his fingertips, incinerating the arrows in mid-flight and killing everyone they touched. Briana couldn't believe how fast he was, even with one hand clasping his necklace.

"Bree, move!" Hamish grabbed her hand and dragged her along. She pulled out of his grasp, but turned her back on Cadeyrn and ran behind the others, following Alasdair along a path to a chapel. They ran inside and Briana, the last in, closed the door and leaned against it, breathing heavily.

"Lady Briana, Lord Hamish, you two must escape the castle or Cadeyrn will kill you, and that will be very, very bad for the future of the world. Let me think, let me think. Riffle to the Riffle Room? No, then 1513 will seal itself. What about back to, no, that wouldn't work either, too advanced. Oh, I know, I know, quick, Glynian, we need one of those arrows."

The cluricaun opened the door a crack, and after a quick peek nipped out and returned within seconds clutching an arrow, which he handed to Alasdair. He, in turn, passed it to Briana.

"Okay, this will get you out of here, make it bigger," the gnome instructed her.

"What?"

"Make the arrow bigger, about the size of a broom. Use your necklace, quick."

"Uhh, okay."

Briana held the arrow with one hand, her necklace with the other. "*Bigger*". With a puff of black smoke the arrow started to grow. When it was the size of a broom, Alasdair told her to stop. Briana let go of her necklace. "Now what?"

"Hold onto it with both hands, no, not in the middle, on

one end. Lord Hamish, do the same on the other end. Good. Now, lift it above your heads and get a good grip. Glynian ..." He looked at Glynian, who opened the door again, and then looked at Briana. "Okay, make it fly."

"What?"

"Fly. It's an arrow, make it fly."

"Oh, umm, fly."

Nothing happened.

"You have to sound like you mean it," Alasdair reminded her, "and you'll have to hold your necklace, but only briefly as you'll need both hands to hold on with."

Briana moved one hand to her necklace, commanded "*Fly*," and then hastily grabbed it again as another puff of black smoke appeared and the arrow started to vibrate. She tightened her grip as the arrow lifted them off the ground.

"Hold on!" Alasdair called as the arrow headed toward the door, flew through it, and shot out over the grounds of the castle, with the dangling twins holding on till their knuckles turned white. They were soon skimming across the loch, heading east, as the wind whipped their faces and the water below them sprayed their legs.

Briana shouted over the noise of the wind, "A boat would be nice about now."

"What?" Hamish shouted back.

"A BOAT – aaaarrrgghh!" In a puff of black smoke, the arrow they were desperately holding on to turned into a small boat. The twins hit the surface with a splash, and as their already heavy medieval coats filled with water they were dragged down.

Briana thrashed about trying to get loose, but continued to

sink, and began to panic. She had a momentary vision of a gravestone, carved with the words, 'Here lies Briana Ryan, born 1994, died 1513', and then Hamish was there.

He and his friends spent so many hours doing underwater training with rocks at the Mount beach for when they came off their boards and were pinned by large waves that he never panicked in water. He had shaken off his coat almost before they hit the surface, dived down to Briana, tore her coat off, and towed her back to the surface.

The little wooden boat the arrow had turned into had landed right side up, and they gratefully scrambled into it. Briana lay in the bottom of the boat, exhausted, shivering, soaking wet, and freezing cold. She began coughing up water.

As Hamish shook the last of the water out of his ears, he said, "Well, I'm glad you didn't scream out Loch Ness Monster or something. But how did you make this happen? You weren't holding your necklace, were you?"

"No, so how did . . ." She looked at Hamish with an expression of horror on her face.

"What?" he cried, jerking his head around. "Llewellyn?"

"Rashid," she cried and burst into tears. "Oh (sob) how (sob) could (sob, sob) how could I (sob) have forgotten (sob) him (sob, sob, sob)?"

Hamish put his arm around her, somewhat awkwardly not being one for cuddles. "I'm sure he'll be okay, Bree. He, well, oh, where was he?"

Briana sniffed. "He-he jumped off my lap when Cadeyrn blasted the door apart in the cellar. It all happened so fast, I ran, I didn't think (sob) I didn't think about him. Oh, how could I?" She buried her face in her brother's shoulder and threw her arms around him.

Hamish patted her on the back. "Look, he's quick, I'm sure he scampered to safety and he'll be fine. Llewellyn isn't after him, he's after us, or rather, after you." He firmly removed Briana's arms from around his neck.

"But why?" she sniffed, hugging herself instead. "Alasdair said Cadeyrn waited till that friend of his had the Elixir, and then killed him. He must be after our Elixir, so what's the point in killing us now, before we have it?"

"I have no idea, but for now our priority is to get to safety. If Llewellyn comes looking for us we're gonna be pretty obvious out here on the loch."

Hamish picked up the oars lying in the bottom of the boat, fitted them in the oarlocks, and started rowing for the eastern shore, while Briana sobbed quietly to herself, worried sick and guilty about Rashid. Some mother she was.

At the shore Hamish beached the boat and helped Briana, still crying, out onto the rocks. The thick vegetation grew from the banks almost to the water. Briana stood there shivering in her wet pyjamas as an icy wind blew around them. The rocks on the shore dug painfully into her bare feet.

"Bree, can you do something about these?" Hamish asked, indicating his wet clothes. "Can you say 'dry' and 'warm' or something and see what happens?"

Briana wiped her hair out of her face, concentrated, held her necklace, and pointed at Hamish. "*Dry warm clothes.*"

"What the? Bree, stockings and a dress were not what I had in mind. Get me out of these, right now."

Briana laughed. She had dressed Hamish in light grey hose and a doublet made of thick wool that looked like a huge puffy coat and came down to just above his knees. The left half was light brown, the right was dark brown, and it had a maroon collar. She had also clad him with stout dark brown leather boots and a woolly maroon hat. She'd been thinking, as she uttered her command, of a picture of a pageboy in a book her friend Natalie had on medieval life, and Hamish was now wearing that outfit.

She shivered again, but not from the cold this time. Did the necklace know what she was thinking? How was that possible?

"Get me out of these bloody girls' clothes!"

Concentrating on her own clothes, Briana clasped her necklace. "*Dry* . . . no, that won't be any good, ah, okay, *dry, warm clothes.*" In another flash of black smoke, she dressed herself in a plain black tracksuit, with her Reebok joggers.

"What the hell? Me, my clothes, Briana." Hamish paused. "What wouldn't have been any good?".

"I was thinking of the dress that Natalie wore to the Medieval Festival in Taupo last year, but if we have to get through that," she pointed at the thick vegetation, "I don't want to be wearing an ankle-length dress, so I thought of my tracksuit instead."

"Is that how it works? The Atlas makes what you're thinking of?".

"How can a book know what I'm thinking? I'm thankful it worked, however it worked, but I don't care how it worked."

"You don't care how? And you call yourself a scientist? Briana, this is so exciting, look, try it again on me, cos I swear, if you don't get me out of these clothes I will chuck you back in the loch. Try it again and think of ..."

He was interrupted by the sound of three phphts from the bushes on the bank, which were accompanied by 'ouches' and other cries of pain, together with a flash of green smoke. There was a scuffle, and Alasdair's voice shouted, "Get off me you big babaloo!"

"Och, you regolithic, ouch, idiot, ouch, you riffle like that and call me a babaloo? Riffling us in tae a thorn bush, indeed. Owwww."

Rashid scampered out of the bushes and jumped into Briana's arms. She hugged him close, started sobbing again, and begged his forgiveness, until she was distracted by the sight of Alasdair sliding and rolling down the hill, closely followed by Glynian who landed on top of him.

Alasdair threw the cluricaun to the side. "Get off me."

Hamish looked quizzically at Alasdair. "Where did you two come from?"

"My Riffle Room."

"Your what?"

"Explanations in a moment, Lord Hamish, but first we have to get out of view."

He pointed his finger at the ground, while clasping his necklace. "*Riffle cellar.*" With a puff of black smoke a set of stairs appeared that descended into the ground. Alasdair pointed at the boat Hamish had beached. "*Revert.*" The gnome picked up the normal-sized arrow now lying there, and disappeared down the stairs.

Briana, carrying Rashid on one hip, followed Alasdair, as did the others. "*Trapdoor,*" Alasdair's voice called and the entrance sealed shut behind them.

They were in a small room, with lots of little rugs

(Peruvian, Alasdair told Briana) and squashy cushions (Turkish). There were torches (Arabian) burning on the walls and a low sit-down table (Japanese) laden with food (Western).

The twins eyed the spread of bacon, eggs, mushrooms, hash browns, and toast. Alasdair conjured steaming mugs of hot chocolate for them all, and handed a cup to Hamish. "You're looking sartorially medieval, my Lord."

"Oh, yeah, damn it, Bree, get me out of this crap."

"How?"

"Think of something else, and try that. That's how the necklace works, isn't it?" he asked Alasdair.

The gnome nodded.

Briana clasped her necklace, and gestured. "*Clothes.*"

There was a faint puff of black smoke, followed by Hamish's angry shout, "BRIANA."

Alasdair, Glynian, and Rashid collapsed laughing. Hamish was now wearing a shocking pink mini-skirt, a pink boob tube, high-heeled pink stilettos, and a blonde, shoulder-length curly wig topped by an enormous flowery hat.

"DAMN IT, BRIANA, THIS IS NOT FUNNY!"

"Sorry, couldn't resist. *Clothes.*"

This time, without any smoke at all, Hamish found himself dressed in a pair of Quiksilver board shorts and a plain white T-shirt. "Quiksilver? What the hell? Briana, how could you? I'd rather wear the pink outfit."

"Why? I was thinking of that poster of the surfer on your bedroom door at home, What's wrong with that?"

"Nothing, if I was Ross Clarke-Jones, but I am sponsored by Shark Alley, I can't wear Quiksilver."

"Your sponsors won't notice you're wearing Quiksilver in 1513."

"It's the principle," he replied with a sniff.

"Oh for goodness sake. What do you want?"

"Give me my Shark Alley jeans, and my black 'The Angels have the Phonebox' sweat-shirt."

Briana obliged, again with no signs of smoke.

Glynian looked at Hamish's sweatshirt. "Cool, I'll try not to blink."

Hamish laughed.

Briana noticed Alasdair staring at her, his eyes wide.

"What?"

"Umm, nothing," he replied, looking away.

"Dude, have to ask, why did Llewellyn try to kill us back at the castle?" Hamish asked Alasdair. "Wouldn't he want to wait until we have the Elixir?"

Alasdair shook his head. "He has another agenda now, more important than gaining another Elixir, and your deaths would advance his plans."

'I don't see how," Briana disagreed. "And if that's so, why didn't he try to kill us at Dan-yr-Ogof or Abergavenny instead of trying to steal the Atlas?"

"WHAT?"

Briana told him what had happened. Alasdair looked shaken and thought before replying. "At Dan-yr-Ogof the car alarm may have saved you. Cadeyrn isn't VERY familiar with the modern world, and those things are enough to give you a fright when they go off even when you do know what they are, let alone if you've never encountered one before."

"What about Abergavenny? Why didn't he try to kill us at

Tyn-y-Bryn?"

"Erm, I'm not sure," Alasdair replied, before changing the subject. He told them what happened to him and Glynian after the twins left the chapel.

"We went to my Riffle Room, which is a room unaffected by time and inaccessible to Cadeyrn, from where we can see what's going on anywhere and anywhen. We couldn't take you with us, because if Briana, as a Questor, had left 1513 without the Elixir Ingredient, she wouldn't have been able to get back here, since the Elixir Years seal themselves off after a Questor has visited."

"Why?" Briana asked.

"Because you only get one chance to collect each Elixir Ingredient. You may remember from your first reading of the Atlas that once a Questor has passed the Atlas on, they retain the powers they have gained. However, Cadeyrn created a potion to suck my powers from me, to feed off me in a way, when I'm around him, thus doubling his powers while reducing mine to almost nothing. He always drinks it before coming to see me, although that's not often as I've managed to pretty much avoid him over the centuries. But until I can counter his potion, I cannot be around him. That's why Glynian and I left for the Riffle Room."

"Can't you make a potion of your own to suck his powers off him? Wouldn't it work both ways?" Briana asked.

"Yes it would, but the potion he uses involves several human and dragon body organs that have to be removed from the victims while they are still alive."

Briana shuddered.

"You won't be able to use your powers against Cadeyrn

either," Alasdair warned her. "The potion will work against you as well, that's why I had to get you away from him."

"But Briana did use her powers against Llewellyn," Hamish told him. "He shot that purple fire at her and she deflected it, remember?"

Alasdair stared at him.

"Oh, no, hang on, you didn't see it, you were flat on the floor. When you fell over Bree stopped the fire that Llewellyn shot at her with her hands.

"I thought he'd missed."

"No, Bree stopped it. And you say that she can't do anything unless she's holding her necklace, but she wasn't holding her necklace when she stopped the fire, and when we were flying across the loch she changed the arrow into a boat while both hands were on the arrow."

Alasdair and Glynian's eyes both widened. "The Twin Heirs of the Prophecy, aye. Alasdair, my God, it must be the power o' the sorcerer's line in them tha' allows Briana to …"

"The power of the what line?" Hamish interrupted. "The power of the … did you just say 'sorcerer's line'?"

XI: Past the Far End of Weird

Briana was about to comment on that as well when Alasdair spoke, with a sharp look at the cluricaun. "Glynian spoke out of turn. Now is not the time for you to hear about that."

Glynian blushed and looked at his feet. As Hamish started to protest, Alasdair put his hand up. "Lord Hamish, please, I must ask you to be patient. You will hear the whole story, but not right now. I had to get away from Cadeyrn, and as far as I knew Lady Briana wouldn't be able to use her powers around him either. Using the arrow was a simple thing for Briana to do, to get you out of the castle but not out of this time before Cadeyrn got close again"

"If you can riffle through the fabric of time and space, couldn't you, or Briana, have translocated us?"

"With Cadeyrn close I didn't have enough power to riffle the two of you anywhere, and Briana is not ready to try something like that."

"What do you mean, not ready?" Hamish asked.

"How long did it take you to learn how to ride a pushbike?"

"I dunno, maybe . . . oh, I get it. Learning how to riffle properly takes time, yeah, like learning how to ride a bike?"

Glynian added, "Some people still need their training wheels on even after a few hunner years." He grinned at Alasdair.

"Yes, well," Alasdair muttered and gave an embarrassed cough. "You might have noticed that when I riffle it's instant, whereas when you riffled here from Abergavenny you dissolved slowly into smoke, is that right?"

"Yup."

"And when Briana first used the Atlas, when she created the torches, she created puffs of black smoke, yes?"

"A bit.".

"Well, that's like a teenager learning to drive for the first time who accidentally grinds the gears and lays down a cloud of smoke."

As Hamish laughed, Briana narrowed her eyes at him. "Do you mind? Besides, I didn't create any smoke when I changed your clothes."

"I know, and that's exciting," Alasdair told her. "You seem to have a natural talent for using the Atlas beyond anything I've seen."

Briana frowned. "But, Alasdair, you disappeared in green smoke from our farm in New Zealand, and from the Information Centre in Abergavenny, and from Tyn-y-Bryn that first night I saw you, and Cadeyrn disappears in purple smoke. I'm sure you've both had lots of practice."

Alasdair blushed. "Ah, yes, well, umm, you see ..." His

obvious embarrassment caused Glynian to laugh. Alasdair sighed. "Oh, all right, I'll admit it, I'm not that good at riffling. I have to concentrate hard to not produce the smoke, so it's easier to let it smoke."

"So, if Llewellyn blows purple smoke, he can't be that good either?" Hamish asked.

"No, he's very, very good. He just likes to show off," Alasdair replied.

"How is displaying your 'training wheels' showing off?"

Alasdair laughed. "He doesn't see it like that. It's more like the example I used before of grinding the gears on a car. Generally, once people can drive properly they stop grinding the gears and laying down smoke. But if they are part of a social group who thinks it's cool, like boy racers, they'll deliberately lay down smoke again. Burnouts, aren't they called?"

Hamish laughed. "So, you're saying Llewellyn is a boy racer?"

"Well, he does like to show off."

"How come his smoke is purple and yours is green and ours was blue?" Briana asked.

Alasdair frowned. "I'm not sure how he does that. As far as I knew there were only four colours associated with the Atlas. Three when riffling: blue if you're moving backward in time, red if you're moving forward, and green if you're moving in space but not in time. Black if you're not riffling but using the powers of the Atlas, like when you made the torches. I don't know how Cadeyrn manages purple, and I don't know what it means, or even if it means anything, that he can. It might be like a boy racer painting his car an unusual colour to stand out from his mates Anyway, back to what I was saying earlier. Lady Briana, if you had tried riffling from one side of the loch to the other when you're so new to the Atlas you could have ended up anywhere or anywhen. The current Questor only has one chance in each time period to gain an Elixir Ingredient, so if I had riffled you out of here, or Briana had inadvertently riffled to another time, her Quest would have been over before it began."

He indicated Rashid, who had been eating non-stop since they had been reunited and hadn't uttered so much as a word.

"Despite being weakened by Cadeyrn, I did manage to riffle back to the cellar to collect Rashid and riffled him back to the Riffle Room. By the time I tuned in on you, you were already in that little boat and seemed to be safe for the moment, so I switched over to watch Cadeyrn."

"What do you mean 'tuned in on us' and 'switched over to watch Cadeyrn'?" Hamish asked.

"We could see you from the Riffle Room. I'll show you what I mean when I take you there, it will be easier than explaining it now. We saw Cadeyrn kill a lot of soldiers, but finally he took an arrow in the heart."

"So he's dead?" Hamish asked. "That's a relief."

Alasdair shook his head. "No, he's Immortal, remember? However, when Immortal Questors are 'killed' they are riffled back to the year they drank the Elixir, where they take a week to recover from the ordeal."

"So, has he been riffled back to 675, when he drank the Elixir, or to 655, where his past self who killed his future self now lives?" Hamish asked.

"He drank the Elixir in 676," Alasdair corrected. "He

started his Quest in 675. But no, he's gone back to 655 since he wiped out his later timeline. It's good news for us - now that he has been 'killed' in 1513, he won't be able to return to this time, because if he does as soon as he riffles in, the arrow in his heart will be there again, he'll be 'killed' again, he'll be returned to his own time again, and he'll take another week to recover from his 'death', which is not a pleasant thing. It's happened to me a few times." He shuddered.

"How many times have you been 'killed'?" Hamish asked.

"I'd rather not talk about it," Alasdair replied stiffly. "Anyway, once Cadeyrn had returned to his own time we riffled in again to where you were." Glynian snorted at this. "Well, all right," Alasdair amended, "almost to where you were. We all make mistakes."

"Every time," Glynian muttered under his breath.

Briana had several questions about what the gnome had told them. "But Alasdair, if you can do all this stuff," she waved her hand around the cellar, "how come you didn't tell us before? And why didn't you make the arrow bigger? How come you made me do it all? I mean, it was a life and death situation back there, not the best time for me to be learning how to use the Atlas, was it?"

"I apologise for that, My Lady, but when you first use the Atlas, you have to completely believe that what you are trying to do must be done. It's the key to unleashing your power. If you'd known I could do these things, you might not have felt you had to, and so it wouldn't have worked, even if I told you my powers were weakened by Cadeyrn's presence. Now your powers have been unleashed, you can use them anytime because you already know you can do it."

Hamish had a half-smile on his face. "That sounds awfully similar to the Eddingses' Theory."

"Similar, yes."

"But they said the person doing the 'magic' has to believe it will work, not that it has to be done. Bree hasn't believed in anything since we left Abergavenny, I doubt she believed that this would work, did you Bree?"

Briana shook her head.

"I agreed it is similar to the Eddingses' Theory, yes, but different too, obviously, or it wouldn't have worked."

"But what about the torches?" Hamish pointed out. "Bree didn't have to make them, so … oh, right, anger?"

"Anger can be a trigger too, whether you believe in the 'magic' or not."

Alasdair changed the subject. "We're safe here now that Cadeyrn has been sent back to 655 for at least a week, so we should go and see if we can't find the Loch Ness Monster so you can collect your first Ingredient. I've never seen the monster myself, well, monsters I should say, obviously there's more than one, but I have it on good authority from friends who have seen them that they are plesiosaurs."

"I don't suppose it would do me any good to tell you the dinosaurs are all extinct?" Briana asked.

"None at all" Alasdair replied. "Now then, does anyone have any idea about the geography of the loch?"

"It's a hundred and sixty kilometres long," Briana began.

"How much is that in miles?" Glynian interrupted.

"About a hundred. It's around one point six kays, or just under a mile wide on average, and for the most part it's around one hundred and eighty metres deep, or five hundred and ninety feet."

Glynian looked impressed. "You're doing those calculations in your head?"

"I like maths. In one place you only have to go fifteen metres out from the shore to find that the water is almost a hundred and fifty metres deep."

"How much …?"

"Sorry, fifty feet out it's five hundred feet deep, so it drops off sharply. The present-day loch, well, present in our time, is around ten thousand years old and dates from the end of the last Ice Age, but the trench-like fault that contains the loch is over four hundred million years old."

"How do you know all this?" Alasdair asked.

"I did a school project on the Loch Ness Monster last year to scientifically disprove it could exist. Isn't that ironic? Anyway, the plesiosaurs lived from the early Jurassic to the late Cretaceous periods, around one hundred and eighty to sixty-five million years ago. They weren't technically dinosaurs, they were a marine reptile with flippers, about twelve metres long, or forty feet for Glynian, with necks that made up half the length of the animal. They had four flippers, sharp teeth set in strong jaws, and a short pointed tail. They ate fish and other swimming animals, and the females laid eggs in the sand, like turtles do."

"You so should have used a David Attenborough accent," Hamish told her. She ignored him.

"You are right, Lady Briana, that the plesiosaurs lived hundreds of millions of years ago, but what you don't know is their descendants have been living here in the loch ever since. They've remained almost unchanged since that time, although evolution has led them to being smaller than their ancestors, about thirty feet in length. They also have much larger eyes to see in the dark waters of the loch, and their necks are not nearly as long as they used to be.

"Not so long ago, well, not 'not so long ago' here in 1513, but 'not so long ago' from your time, a huge underwater cavern was discovered in the loch, which led to a network of caves. I believe the Loch Ness Monsters are guarding the Elixir Ingredient in one of these caves."

Briana shook her head in disagreement. "I remember the discovery, well, not when it happened obviously, I was too young, but I came across it when I was researching my project. The scientists never found any signs of life there."

"They didn't look in the right places, My Lady," Alasdair told her. "Now, obviously we can't swim to the caves in a freezing cold loch so we'll take a submarine."

"A submarine? I suppose you happen to have one on you, do you?" Hamish asked.

"I do as a matter of fact." Alasdair stood and walked toward the staircase. Opening the trapdoor with a command, he disappeared up the stairs, followed by Glynian. Briana wasn't showing any signs of moving. She was slowly stroking Rashid, who had fallen asleep on her lap after he'd finished eating.

Hamish walked past her. "Come on Bree, and wake the fuzz bucket up."

"Hamish, we're going into Loch Ness? In a submarine? In 1513? To look for a plesiosaur?"

"Hell yeah, come on, it'll be awesome."

"Hamish, I can't ... we can't ... this isn't ... oh man, if I say 'one, two, three, wake up' will it help?"

"Not in the slightest." Hamish bounded up the stairs.

Briana woke Rashid up. "Come on, little one, let's go and do something else impossible, shall we?" Rashid threw his paws around Briana's neck, and the two of them followed the others.

Alasdair was waiting for them at the top, while Glynian and Hamish were already standing on the shores of the loch. As Briana and Rashid left the cellar and walked to the shore, Alasdair clasped his necklace and pointed at the cellar. "*Riffle off.*" It disappeared in a cloud of black smoke.

"Boy racer," Hamish teased him.

"Training wheels is more like it," Glynian stated with a grin.

"Where did it go?" Briana asked.

"Into a storage riffle."

"Oh."

Alasdair joined the others at the side of the loch, and pulled out a small model of a submarine from a pocket of his trousers, which he placed in the water. Hamish laughed and smacked the top of it, forcing it underwater.

"Dude, unless you have some fancy Time Lord science tucked away in this little thing we won't all squeeze in there."

"Not Time Lord science, advanced enlargement technology. Don't hit it like that, it's fragile in this state." Alasdair gave the sub a gentle nudge and sent it floating out to deeper water. "*Larger*," he commanded, holding his necklace and pointing at the sub, which grew until it was the size of a large van, emitting enormous billows of black smoke as it did so.

"Just big enough for the five of us. Come on."

"You weren't breathing heavily after making that riffle cellar," Briana commented.

"No, but that didn't involve, oh, it was just different. I'm too out of breath to explain it right now."

"What are we supposed to do? Swim out to it?" Hamish asked.

"Of course not. *Visible*," Alasdair commanded. A little jetty appeared in front of them, extending from the shore to the sub. Alasdair did a few more commands and gestures to align the sub with the jetty, and secure it. He led the others out onto the jetty, climbed down the little ladder, and disappeared through the hatch, followed by the others.

There were four seats inside (Rashid sat on Briana's lap), and lots of gadgets and gizmos on the control panel.

"Where did that jetty come from?" Hamish asked. "And won't people see it now?"

"Oh, yes, I forgot that. *Invisible*," Alasdair commanded. "I put the jetty there ages ago as Glynian and I come here occasionally for the fishing. It's great for salmon and trout.'

"What if someone walks into it?" Briana asked.

"There are wards on it."

Briana was a bit dubious, but didn't argue the point. "What did you mean by 'enlargement technology'? You can't tell me turning that model into a real submarine was technology, surely that was magic?"

"As I've said before My Lady, while it may appear as magic to you, in reality it's advanced technology."

Briana raised one eyebrow.

"Have you ever needed to reduce or enlarge an image on a photocopier?"

"Of course, but …"

"Well, this is the same thing."

"The same thing? How is turning a model submarine into a real submarine the same thing as using a photocopier?"

"It wasn't a model, it was a real submarine reduced down. Obviously the technology is a little more advanced than your average copy machine uses, but the principle is the same."

Briana was still dubious. "Let's say I believe that, which I don't, where did the technology come from?"

"I, err, need to get the sub ready to dive now, My Lady." Alasdair turned his attention to the controls.

Briana exchanged an exasperated glance with Hamish, who considered Alasdair for a moment, then shook his head slightly. Briana sighed knowing Hamish was right. They wouldn't get anything out of the stubborn gnome that he didn't want to tell them.

"Where did you learn how to navigate a sub?" Briana asked instead.

"During World War II, My Lady. I disguised myself as a human dwarf and joined the Navy."

Briana wondered about that. "Didn't they, umm, have, ahh, a height restriction for joining the Navy back then?"

Alasdair smiled and touched his necklace. "I encouraged the humans to overlook a few regulations."

"Actually, I've used this particular sub before during my travels. It even survived an attack by an Ahuizotl once in South America. Fearsome creature. Eats fishermen, you know. I collected the sub from the Riffle Room after we left Urquhart Castle."

He guided the little sub out into the loch, toward the east, until the sonar gauge said they were over the deepest part.

"Okay, prepare to dive." Punching buttons and pushing levers, he frowned at a red light flashing on the console, before turning and narrowing his eyes at Hamish. "You must have broken the hatch automation when you hit the sub. You'll have to go and close it by hand."

Hamish grumbled, but climbed the little ladder to the sub's hatch and stuck his head out.

"Hey, cool," his voice floated down to the others. "The castle looks great from out ... oh wow! You're kidding me, oh, totally, totally way, way, way past the far end of weird. It is a plesiosaur, fantastic! Bree, get up here, you gotta see this. it's coming this way. Bree, get up here now, the Loch Ness Monster does exist! This is incredible, a real-life dinosaur is living in ... hey, where did it go? It dived. I can't see it."

Alasdair was yelling at Hamish to get inside when Briana saw Hamish's feet disappear off the ladder, followed by his scream and a tremendous splash.

Without consciously thinking about it, Briana threw her arms upwards and cried out, "*Shark suit!*" She then scrambled up the ladder.

The Loch Ness Monster had surfaced next to the sub, grabbed Hamish in its mouth, and plunged back into the dark waters of the ice-cold loch.

XII: A Killer called Kenai

Briana was staring at the surface of the water when Alasdair's head appeared out of sub's hatch.

"Where's Kenai?"

"Kenai?"

"Your toy killer whale, quick, where is he?"

"In Hamish's wardrobe. We locked all my stuff …"

Before Briana could say anything else Alasdair held his necklace and riffled out in a puff of red smoke. Seconds later he reappeared with a 'phpht' in blue smoke, accompanied by the sound of an enormous splash outside the submarine. Alasdair climbed out the hatch and joined Briana on the deck of the sub.

"The plesiosaur, it's back, it's resurfaced." Briana cast a desperate glance around the loch.

"No, Lady Briana, that was Kenai."

"What do you mean that was Kenai?"

"I went back to the Riffle Room and used my Riffle Computer to check on your house to make sure your cousin or uncle weren't there, riffled into Hamish's bedroom, broke into his wardrobe, don't worry, I relocked it after I'd finished, took Kenai, and riffled back to the Riffle Room. I explained to Kenai what was going on, and then . . ."

"What do you mean you explained to Kenai?"

Alasdair threw a meaningful glance at Rashid, who had just bounced through the hatch.

"Oh."

"I explained to Kenai what was going on, we riffled back here and Kenai has now gone to rescue Hamish for us." He paused. "Hopefully," he added.

"Hopefully?"

"Well, Kenai will do his best, but we can't be sure."

"We can't . . . THAT IS MY BROTHER OUT THERE IN THE JAWS OF A PLESIOSAUR! Why can't you go back to before it happened? You could pull him inside and shut the hatch before the monster has a chance to take him."

"No, My Lady. If I was to appear earlier than when I left, there would be two Alasdairs. Trust me – you never, ever, ever, want to meet yourself whilst traveling in time. You must not be seen."

"My brother has been taken by a plesiosaur and you're quoting Dumbledore at me?"

"I quote the truth where I find it."

"Whatever. What else can we do for Hamish?"

"There's nothing else we can do. We have to wait and hope that Kenai can rescue him." He looked at her quizzically. "What did you call out just before Hamish was taken?" It sounded like 'Shiatzu' or something."

"Oh, shark suit. I watched a documentary recently about

sharks, and the divers had these cool shark armour suits on."

"You may just have saved your brother's life. If he hasn't drowned, that is."

Briana's eyes filled with tears, and she turned away from the gnome, picking Rashid up for comfort. The three of them balanced on the top deck of the submarine, watching the dark waters of the loch.

"Kenai will save him, Mum."

"Actually," Alasdair said, "It took a bit of convincing to get Kenai to come along. He seemed content to let your brother drown."

"What the hell?"

"Apparently Hamish used to be mean to Kenai and the rest of your toys when you weren't around. Kenai said Hamish used to go into your room and try to staple his fins together, pull Poppadom's tusks out, or pull Ryszard's wings off."

"When was this?"

"Oh, years ago, when he was about five or six. He's probably forgotten all about it, but I suspect the animals never will, especially Poppadom. You know what they say about elephants. Actually, I don't think it was to save your brother that Kenai finally agreed to come."

"Then why did he come?"

"He's hoping to bag a plesiosaur for his dinner."

Briana shuddered.

Out on the loch the water started to churn as the monster's head and neck broke the surface, with Hamish still in its mouth. Hamish managed to scream once before the monster dived again, followed by a flick of Kenai's tail.

Briana's stomach clenched and a weight settled in her chest. Alasdair placed a comforting hand on her arm, but Briana hardly noticed.

After nearly two minutes, Kenai reappeared with Hamish astride his back, clutching the orca's dorsal fin and gulping deep breaths of air as they broached the surface.

Briana gave a cry of joy . Alasdair was obviously impressed at the length of time Hamish had been underwater. "I can't believe he held his breath so long, that's incredible."

Kenai positioned himself next to the sub, Hamish scrambled off the whale and onto the deck, and Briana threw her arms around him, after putting Rashid down.

"Oh Hamish, I thought you'd drowned, I thought we'd lost you."

Hamish disentangled himself from her embrace, and laughed in a mix of shock and exhilaration. "I'm fine, Bree, thanks to you, and that orca. Quick thinking with the shark suit ... look ... not even a scratch!" He laughed. "I figured all that underwater rock training me and my mates do on flat days at the Mount beach would come in handy one day, but I was thinking more along the lines of if I ever get pinned by a big wave at Teahupo'o, not taken under Loch Ness by a plesiosaur." He shook himself, and shivered. "Sheesh, that's even colder than the time I went surfing the Caitlins in winter. Can someone dry me off please?"

Using his necklace, Alasdair obliged.

"Are you sure you're okay?" Briana asked Hamish.

"I'm fine, Bree, don't worry about me. What a rush!"

"In that case ..." Briana pushed him so hard with both hands he lost his balance and fell into the loch again. He surfaced, spluttering. "What the hell? Wotcha do that for?"

"All those horrible things I've found out you did to my toys!"

"What horrible things?"

"Trying to staple Kenai's fins together, trying to pull Poppodom's tusks out, trying to . . ."

"Bree, for God's sake, that was years ago. And how was I supposed to know they were real? Would be real. Are real. Whatever." He hauled himself out of the loch and onto the sub's platform. "Alasdair, sorry, d'ya mind again?" Alasdair dried him off with a slight smile.

"So, that orca that saved me, that's your toy orca from back home, yeah?"

"The one you kick, yeah, yeah, the one you hit, yeah, yeah, the one you punch, yeah, yeah," Kenai sang, loudly and tunelessly.

"Look, dude, sorry about that, but it was years ago, I was just a kid, and besides, the thought that you'd be alive one day never even crossed my mind."

Kenai, debated the matter in his mind. "Hmmm, I still think I should've left you for monster fodder, dude. Still, if you're a surfer, I guess you can't be all bad."

"I'm really, really sorry. No hard feelings?" He offered his palm.

Kenai gave him a high five with one of his fins. "Sweet, man, we're cool. Now, speaking of monster fodder . . . I'm gonna go see if I can't catch me a bite. Outta here." The orca dived, and disappeared with a flick of his tail.

Alasdair gestured towards the ladder. "Okay, now that Hamish is safe let's go and see if we can't find these caves."

He directed them into the sub, followed them, and closed the hatch behind them.

Glynian moved into the co-pilot's seat, turning the controls back over to Alasdair, and soon the little sub was deep under the surface of Loch Ness. Alasdair pointed to a screen. "The sonar will tell us where the caves are and show us any plesiosaurs that happen to be around. Oh, look." He tapped at two shapes that had appeared on the screen. "There's Kenai chasing a plesiosaur."

They scanned the bottom of the loch for a good hour before Alasdair found an enormous tunnel in the vertical rock wall of the loch. He manoeuvred the sub along the tunnel, eventually surfacing in an underwater cavern. After opening the hatch he led them up the ladder and onto the sub's deck.

The cavern was enormous, and eerily lit with some kind of phosphorescence. Briana wondered how fresh air managed to get into it, but presumed there must be air tunnels running to the surface somewhere. The walls of the cavern looked nastily jagged, and there were loose rocks on the floor.

Kenai emerged next to the sub and aimed his waterspout right at Hamish, soaking him through. Alasdair laughed, and looked at Briana. "Your turn."

"What?"

"To dry Hamish off."

"Oh, okay," she held her necklace and commanded, "*Dry*."

"Thanks, Bree." He turned back to the killer whale. "You said no hard feelings."

"Just messing with ya, dude."

Alasdair headed off any further quibbles by pointing to a

tunnel leading out of the cavern where a red glow was pulsing like a heartbeat. "Look over there."

Briana took a step forward. "What is it?"

"It's an Elixir Ingredient, they all glow like that."

"There ain't no jetty here dude, how do we get ashore?"

"Yeah, about that, ahh, we'll have to swim. Briana and I can dry everyone off once we get out of the water."

Hamish rolled his eyes, but jumped into the water and swam ashore. Briana followed, shocked at how cold the water was. She quickly dried herself, Hamish, and Rashid with a word, while Alasdair did the same for himself and Glynian.

Rashid, in particular, had not enjoyed the short swim, and started on a tirade as soon as Briana had dried him.

"Well, that should attract the plesiosaurs quicker than anything," Hamish commented wryly. Rashid stopped mid-sentence, and put his paws over his mouth.

Hamish patted the monkey's head. "Good boy."

Briana found she had to walk carefully through the cavern as the loose rocks kept shifting under her feet, and several times she nearly fell. She was relieved to reach the tunnel. "At least we can use the walls to balance ourselves now."

However, when Glynian tripped and caught himself on the wall, he let out a cry of pain. He held up his palm and Briana was surprised to see bright yellow blood.

"I dinnae suggest touchin' these walls," he advised, wiping his hand on his apron, "it's like touchin' a razor."

As they followed the tunnel, the pulsing red glow gradually became brighter. After emerging into a smaller cavern without any phosphorescence, Briana could see a pedestal standing in the centre. Intricately carved with Celtic-looking designs, it supported a red velvet cushion with silver trimmings and tassels. Sitting on this cushion was a beautiful little heart-shaped bottle, which was producing the pulsing red light. Alasdair told Briana what to do.

"Clasp your necklace, My Lady, and take the bottle."

"What would happen if I didn't have my hand on the necklace when I tried to take it?"

"Actually, I'm not sure. I mean, generally the Atlas protects its Ingredients against non-Questors by killing anyone who tries to take one without holding an Atlas necklace, but because of who you are it might not kill you. Still, better safe than sorry, I would suggest."

Briana swallowed. She clasped her necklace tightly and took the bottle off its cushion. As she did so, the cavern echoed with what sounded like the angry roaring of a thousand lions.

"What the hell is that?" Hamish asked.

"That would be the plesiosaurs," Alasdair replied. "They'll try to stop us getting away with the Elixir Ingredient."

"Now you tell us?"

"Run," Alasdair cried, taking off and leaving the others to follow.

Running through the tunnel, Briana tried desperately not to trip, with the screams of the plesiosaurs echoing all around. It wasn't easy as the loose rocks kept shifting under her feet.

"Head for the sub," Alasdair cried as they burst into the cavern. "Kenai, we need you, *now*," he called as a herd of plesiosaurs swam into the main cavern and headed toward the group running for the sub. Alasdair was running out in front, and as he ran he touched his necklace with one hand and gestured to the sub saying, "*Revert.*"

"What are you doing?" Hamish screamed as the sub shrank to its toy size in a cloud of black smoke, and bobbed in the water close to the shore.

Alasdair ignored him, plunged into the water, pocketed the sub, and raced back out of the water, as Kenai, with an enormous leap, beached himself.

"Everybody hold hands, Rashid, go to Briana, Hamish take Kenai's fin." Hamish looked warily at the killer whale. "Hurry," Alasdair cried.

As Briana clung to Rashid's paw with her right hand, Glynian took her left as a plesiosaur, its gaping mouth displaying a set of gleaming teeth, leapt for her.

XIII: Parallel Harry

Briana screamed as Alasdair cried out, "*Riffle Room.*" The plesiosaur's jaws snapped shut on empty air as Briana found herself transported into a tunnel of stars like the one that had brought her to Scotland in 1513, except that this one was green, not blue.

This tunnel phphted her onto a black leather couch, one of several positioned around a dark wooden coffee table that Glynian landed on. Observing the huge room around her, it looked to Briana like a Victorian library.

Over to her left, Alasdair had phphted onto the floor in front of a wall with a double window set into it, next to a table and chairs. The other walls were all filled with bookshelves. Behind her a spiral staircase led to a second level, also entirely given over to bookshelves, which rose to a magnificent stained glass dome.

Rashid and Hamish were on the second level, where Rashid was perched on a banister. He waved a paw at Briana, and she waved back. "Are you okay?" He gave her a paws up.

She was about to tell him to come down when she heard a loud splash from outside the room. She turned her head in time to see a sheet of water entirely cover the windows. Presumably there was a pool or lake outside the window and Kenai had phphted into it. That was a relief. With Alasdair's self-confessed misguided aims when riffling, he might have dropped Kenai in the library.

Hamish was looking wide-eyed. "Oh my gosh, I don't believe it. We're in the library at the Skywalker Ranch. Oh, totally wicked, man. How do you know George? Where is he? Wow, what an honour, I can't wait to meet him." Hamish took the stairs two at a time and headed for the door.

"Sorry to disappoint you, Lord Hamish, but we're not at the Skywalker Ranch."

"Of course we are. I've seen photos of it and this is definitely the Skywalker Ranch library." He paused. "Or a damn fine copy."

"Actually," Alasdair informed him, "the Skywalker Ranch library is a damn fine copy, as you put it, of my library. George liked it and asked if he could use the design."

"So you do know George? And he's been here?"

"Well of course I know him, I gave him half of his ideas. I haven't seen him for several years now. We've been meaning to catch up, but we've both been so busy, although we do keep in touch by e-mail."

"George who?" Briana asked.

Hamish rolled his eyes. "Honestly, Bree, there's fantasilliterate and then there's just plain stupid."

"I am not stupid."

"Oh, come on, even you've heard of *Star Wars*. Skywalker

Ranch is George Lucas's film-makers' retreat."

"Of course I've heard of *Star Wars*, but those of us not obsessed with fantasy don't automatically assume 'George' means George Lucas."

"What, and the 'Skywalker' didn't give it away?"

Briana gave him a blank look.

"Skywalker? Luke Skywalker? Honestly, Bree, it's so embarrassing being related to you sometimes. And Star Wars is sci-fi, not fantasy you idiot." He ignored the look Briana gave him and turned to Alasdair. "So, where exactly are we then?"

"In my Riffle Room, the one I told you about back at the loch."

"I remember. You said it's, what, outside time or something like that?"

"Exactly."

"So, where is it then?"

"Nowhere and everywhere. Outside time and inside all times. Umm, it's a bit hard to explain, really."

Hamish laughed. "Well, wherever, or whenever it is, I'm glad there are no plesiosaurs here. And speaking of them, why didn't you riffle us out straight after we had the Elixir Ingredient? We were nearly monster tucker."

"We couldn't leave without the submarine."

"Why not?"

"We couldn't leave behind riffle remains of a time-continuum-unfriendly substance that could possibly have destroyed the chronologicality of particle discovery."

Hamish blinked. "Didn't quite follow that."

Glynian chuckled. "Aye laddie, me clever wee friend here

dinnae always remember to simplify his explanations for us simple folk. I'm wi' you on the no' understandin'." He paused. "And I do believe he invented sum o' those words. One at least."

Alasdair smiled at him, but didn't reply; instead, he gestured to a cabinet at the far end of the library. "My Lady, you can store the Elixir Ingredient in there. Place the bottle in the top left space; you'll see where it goes."

Walking over to the cabinet, Briana saw on the far left of the top shelf a little round hole cut into the wood, the same size as the base of the bottle.

She carefully took out the Elixir Ingredient, which was no longer pulsating with red light, and placed the bottle in the space Alasdair had indicated.

As she did so, a rectangular plaque appeared on the back of the cabinet behind it.

"What are they?" Briana called down the library.

"What are what?" Alasdair called back.

"The runes, I don't recognise them, they don't look the same as the ones in the Atlas."

"Oh, no, they're not, they're the Angerthas runes."

"The what?"

"Angerthas runes. Tolkien invented them. For some reason the plaques for the ingredients use them."

"Oh." Briana decided not to ask how that happened. "What do they say?"

"The top ones say *The Elixir Ingredient* and the lower ones, in this case, will say *of the Loch Ness Monster*. The lower runes will change for each ingredient."

Briana looked at the cute drawing of the plesiosaur in the middle of the runes. It was awfully incongruous with the actual creatures that had been so scary in real life. There was also, now, another cut in the wood that had appeared to the right of where the Ingredient bottle was sitting. Presumably it was for the next Ingredient.

After going back to join the others, she found Alasdair explaining to Hamish how the Riffle Computer worked. Hamish was grinning as he waved his hands in the air, moving items around a holographic screen by flicking his fingers. "Bree, this is awesome, it's like Tony Stark's Holo-Computer."

Briana didn't bother to ask who that was, although the holograph reminded her of those on the *CSI* shows her Dad used to watch, so Tony Stark was probably a detective.

From the top of the screen, Briana could see Hamish had selected "present time" from the top of a menu that then ran chronologically backwards, year by year. Did that mean they could look in on different times? The menu ran off the page – she wondered how far back it went.

"Scroll to New Zealand, and flick on it," Alasdair instructed Hamish.

"What's Ahaura?" Briana asked as a menu appeared on-screen.

"A small town on the west coast of the South Island. Scroll to Tauranga, flick on it, scroll to your suburb, and flick on that."

Hamish did so with a twitch of his fingers, the first flick producing a sub-menu of Tauranga suburbs. Once he flicked on 'Te Puna' a list of names and addresses appeared.

"It looks like a phone book," Briana commented.

"A little more advanced, My Lady. Hit 'R,' now scroll to the listing for your name, flick on that."

Hamish did as he was told, and Briana started in surprise as the screen filled with an aerial view of their house in New Zealand.

The menu bar that had shown different years had disappeared, and been replaced by an unusual menu.

ROOF ON	⊗
ROOF OFF	O
OPEN	V
CLOSE	Λ
LAYERS H	≡
LAYERS V	III
ENLARGE	⊕
REDUCE	⊖

Hamish didn't seemed a little disappointed. "Oh, it's the same as Google Earth, then, although I'll grant that the quality is better." He paused. "And more up to date. Google Earth still shows our house with the large tree that came down in a storm two years ago."

Alasdair smiled. "Indeed. And it goes a little further than Google Earth." He waved his hand and produced a menu bar that appeared down the left side of the screen.

"Flick on 'Roof Off'," Alasdair told Hamish.

Hamish did so, and Briana gasped as the roof disappeared. She could now see *into* their house.

"The rest of the buttons are fairly self-explanatory. You can open and close drawers, cupboards, closets, and so on, enlarge or reduce the picture to see something clearer."

Hamish started doing that, and now looked more impressed.

Alasdair gave another instruction. "These two options, LAYERS 1 and LAYERS 2, allow you to look through layers of stuff, either horizontally or vertically, like this."

Alasdair moved his fingers slightly and used the buttons to enlarge the picture until the screen only showed Hamish's wardrobe.

With a flick he opened the door of the wardrobe, and at a flick on LAYERS V all the items hanging vertically in the wardrobe appeared to fly out of the wardrobe and arranged themselves in tidy rows and columns across the holographic screen.

"If you want to check out the contents of a drawer where stuff is stacked on top of each other, you use LAYERS H,' Alasdair told Hamish.

Briana had a look of horror on her face, which Alasdair noticed before he said anything else to Hamish.

"What's wrong?"

"Have you ever heard the term 'invasion of privacy'?"

Alasdair sniffed. "Well, obviously one uses one's discretion about what to look at and not look at," he told her. "You'll notice I did not use Hamish's underwear drawer as an example."

Hamish laughed.

"Turn it off," Briana ordered.

Alasdair shut the screen with a sharp twist of his palm.

Briana was furious. "You've been watching us, haven't you? That's how you knew about Kenai, and how you knew where to find me on the farm back home, and at the Information Centre in Abergavenny, and in St. Mary's. How long have you been spying on us? And why?"

Before Alasdair had a chance to answer, Rashid slid down the banister, jumped into Briana's arms, and declared he was hungry. Alasdair hastily suggested that they all head outside where they could have something to eat next to Kenai's pool, and took off almost at a run, leaving Briana fuming behind him as Rashid continued to chatter away at her.

When she followed Alasdair out of the room, intending to pin him down on the subject of spying, she was, instead, distracted by where she found herself.

An enormous garden, bordered by a huge lake, stretched out ahead of her. She looked back, and her stomach lurched. Instead of the house she expected, all she could see was a doorway (the one she had walked out of) suspended against an inky black back-ground of stars.

Briana hastily walked back through the doorway and found herself in the library again. Taking a deep breath, she turned around, and walked back out into the garden. Turning back and looking again, she shuddered. For some reason the image of the door surrounded by the starry Universe gave her the creeps. Almost afraid of what she'd see, she looked up.

The entire garden appeared to be covered by a domed roof built of steel girders and glass panels, beyond appeared to be a sunny, blue sky. She frowned. As impossible as it seemed, it looked familiar. She was almost certain she had seen that domed roof before somewhere.

"You're kidding," Hamish exclaimed. "We're in the Welsh National Botanic Gardens at Cardiff?"

Briana remembered she had collected a brochure from the Abergavenny Tourist Information Centre on the Gardens, but she was surprised Hamish had recognised it; he wasn't the sort to take notice of gardens. When she pointed that out to him, he laughed. *"The Waters of Mars."*

"The what?"

"An episode of *Doctor Who*. They filmed parts of it in the geodesic greenhouse at the Botanic Gardens, which is where we are now."

"Not exactly," Alasdair stated.

Hamish looked at the gnome, back toward the library, and then at Alasdair again. "Don't tell me you also designed the Botanic Gardens in Cardiff?" he asked in disbelief.

"No, no, just the greenhouse, which is a copy of this one here. Now, then, how about some lunch?"

Briana blinked, struggling to keep up with the way Alasdair would casually throw these astonishing bits of information out, and follow them with a mundane comment such as 'How about some lunch?'

She had no idea whether it was lunchtime or not. Her body clock had had enough trouble adjusting from New Zealand to British time, let alone to 1513 and then to no time, or outside time, or wherever or whenever they were now. Still, she was hungry, so she took a seat on one of the outdoor dining chairs and joined the others in the meal Alasdair produced on the table.

"Hey, dudes, what about me?" Kenai called from the lake. "Those overgrown lizards proved to be slippery little suckers. Man, what a feast they would have been. Don't s'pose you can send me back so I can bag one?"

"Sorry, Kenai, we can't go back there, but I can do this." Alasdair clasped his necklace and gestured to the lake. "*Fish.* There you go, you'll find a few schools up the other end."

"Wicked, dude, thanx." Kenai flicked his tail and took off toward the far end of the lake.

"Where's Rashid?" Briana asked.

"Up here, Mum." Rashid was high in the branches of a large tree beside the lake. "Alasdair gave me some bananas, I'm gonna eat them and then have a kip, okay?"

"Okay. Don't fall out of the tree." She laughed at Rashid's indignant snort, and turned back to the meal, raising an eyebrow at Hamish's plate.

Her brother had built himself a five-layer hamburger. "Mixed grill," he grinned at her.

"Sorry?"

Hamish pointed to the layers in turn. "Chicken, beef, bacon, ham, and more bacon."

"And one lettuce leaf?"

"Gotta stay healthy."

Briana rolled her eyes and then turned to Alasdair. She knew from his hasty exit from the library there wouldn't be any point pursuing a discussion about the riffle computer, despite the many questions she still had. Instead, she asked for more information about what he had said earlier about riffle remains.

"Once you have an Elixir Ingredient and return to the Riffle Room, you have to be careful you don't leave anything behind that doesn't belong in that time, things I call riffle remains. You see ..."

"I've heard all this," Glynian interrupted. "Laddie, I don't s'pose a teenager from your time plays backgammon, does he?" he asked Hamish.

"Backgammon? Absolutely," Hamish replied enthusiastically. Despite the hours that Hamish spent on-line gaming, he and Lachlan had also played traditional backgammon and chess for years, and still preferred using boards to computers.

Glynian was delighted. "Fancy a game? Alasdair, could you riffle the set out here? I'm still a little sore from yer terrible riffling tae be getting' up and doon."

"Hamish needs to hear about riffle remains."

"Dude, it's not only girls who can multi-task. I can whip this cluricaun's butt and listen to you at the same time. Let us get started, and then I'll be back with you."

Glynian rubbed his hands in glee. "Ah, laddie, I like a bit o' optimism in me opponents, ill placed as it may be."

Alasdair frowned, but with a word and a gesture he deposited the conjured board on the ground beside them, scattering the pieces everywhere. Glynian glared at him.

"Ya dinnae hae tae do that." He retrieved the board and pieces and placed them on the table.

Alasdair blushed . "I didn't do it on purpose."

Glynian laughed, set the board up, and explained it.

Briana looked at the board. Instead of the geometric triangular shapes on Hamish's board at home, this one was painted in a way that made it look like triangular rocky outcrops. "Strange board," she commented.

"Alasdair bought it in Scandinavia around the time of the Vikings," Glynian told her.

Instead of different colours, the playing pieces were small stones, with different runes carved and painted on them. Glynian passed half of the stones to Hamish.

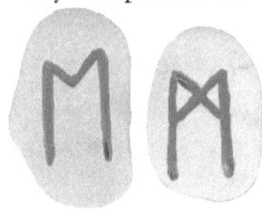

The cluricaun explained them as "Ehwaz, which means horse, and Mannaz, which means man". The explanation didn't help Briana.

"Where are the dice?" Hamish asked.

Glynian laid out twelve further, smaller, stones; six identical pairs.

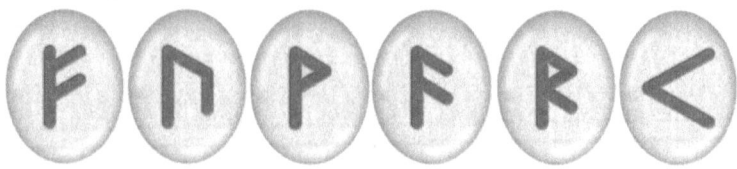

"What are they?" Hamish asked.

"Runes fae the Elder Futhark. Fehu, Uruz, Thurisaz, Ansuz, Raidho, and Kenaz."

"Huh?"

"Cattle, wild ox, thorn tree, divine power, wheel, and knowledge."

"That doesn't help," Hamish said, unknowingly echoing Briana's earlier thought.

"One, two, three, four, five, six. The Futhark is an ancient alphabet. You draw two stones instead o' rolling dice."

"Oh, okay."

Glynian drew two runes and moved a piece with a Quairtra rune, then Hamish moved a Lagus rune.

"Can we please get back to discussing riffle remains?" Alasdair asked. "It is important, you know."

Briana turned back to Alasdair. "Sorry, you were saying?"

"Everything needs to happen in its correctly allotted time frame. A 'time-continuum-unfriendly substance' means a substance left behind in a time before it has been discovered, or invented, like the plastic components in the sub. To leave something like that behind could cause serious problems in the time-space continuum."

"Problems such as what?" Briana asked.

"Well, imagine if the sub had made it to the surface and been found. If someone figured out from it how to make plastic in 1513, the whole course of history could be changed, not to mention the extra mess the world would be in today with another five hundred years of plastic rubbish polluting it."

"Ohhhhh-kay, I get the theory, but it's unlikely anyone would ever have found the sub if you'd left it behind in a cavern under Loch Ness, and less likely they would have worked out what it was made of, and how to make it."

"Maybe that's not the best example. I know, imagine if we'd left it behind and it was dug up in your time and carbon dated. Imagine the furore that would cause amongst the archaeologists in your time. That's why, when riffling out of an Elixir Ingredient's time, we can't leave anything behind."

"Couldn't we have gone back and collected it later?" Briana asked. "When we had about fifty less plesiosaurs trying to kill us?"

Alasdair laughed, and shook his head. "No. Remember when I told you the Elixir Years are sealed in time? You cannot return to a year in which you gained an Elixir Ingredient, except for the year when you acquired the final Ingredient and drank the potion. That year is where you return to recover if you are 'killed', well, if you choose Immortality that is." He paused. "Then again, because you are the . . . never mind. It might work for you, but I'm not absolutely certain."

"What would work?"

"Ah, we'll discuss that later." He took a large bite of his sandwich and refused to discuss the matter further, despite Briana's frustrated attempts to get him to talk.

"Fine," she eventually conceded ungraciously. "Can you tell us some more about K-K-Kdarrin, then?" An unfamiliar shiver of excitement coursed through her when she said his name.

Alasdair mistook her stuttering for struggling with the name itself, not the man. "Cadeyrn. C-a-d-e-y-r-n. It's from the Welsh *cad* meaning 'battle' and *teyrn* meaning 'king' or 'monarch'."

"How do you think C-Cadeyrn is planning to take over the world? If he brings an army to the present from 655, armed with swords and crossbows and stuff, surely today's military would destroy them with Uzis, and AK-47s, and tanks."

"I know that My Lady, and that's not how he plans to do it. He . . ."

"Will work in reverse?" Hamish interrupted, as he waited for Glynian to make a move, showing he was listening to Alasdair. "Take Uzis and AKs back to 655?"

Alasdair shook his head. "No, modern technology doesn't work in the past."

"So how were you able to use the sub in the past?"

"It's different."

"How?"

"It just is." Alasdair's determined tone ended any further discussion, or any hope of an explanation. How could some technology work in the past, while other technology didn't? Briana seethed. Alasdair was so frustrating at times.

The gnome didn't notice her frustration, or at the very least, was pretending not to. "Cadeyrn will work with numbers, build a massive army, and conduct military campaigns in his time using modern strategy. Remember when I said if we change something in history, we'd change the future, including your present? Well, if Cadeyrn can establish himself as a tyrannical dictator in 655, the whole course of history will be changed, and because he's immortal, when you return to your time, he will still be the ruler, and everything will be different.

"The Industrial Revolution, the discovery of electricity, the telephone, and computers all gave power to the masses and improved people's lives. Cadeyrn doesn't want that. If he can win a war in the distant past, when you return to your time, I believe you will find the human race still living much as it did in the seventh century."

Briana considered what Alasdair had said. "It would have to be a world war then, wouldn't it? I mean, if he wins a small battle in Wales in 655, that won't affect the history of the whole world, will it? I can't see how it would affect, say, our New Zealand in the present, or the United States, or China."

"He'll do it gradually; take over one part of the world in 655, see how it affects the present, and then take over another part."

Hamish joined the conversation. "It could be fun, living in a medieval time I mean, although I would miss my computer." He paused. "But then, if it hadn't been invented, I guess I wouldn't miss it because I wouldn't know about it."

Alasdair shook his head. "For the rest of the world that would be true, but not for you, or for us. We would know what the world should have been like because we could still travel in time using these," he touched his necklace. "However, the rest of the world would have no knowledge of what should have been, and would find themselves living a miserable medieval life under an evil dictator."

Briana frowned. "If Cadeyrn is putting together an army of some considerable size, big enough to take over the world, wouldn't it register in our time in the history books? I mean, historical facts from the seventh century are murky, but a big army gathering could still filter through time, couldn't it? If we keep an eye on the internet and then go back to 655 we could do something about it before it gets too big."

Alasdair acknowledged her point. "If it was noticed, yes. But Cadeyrn has the entire army camped within the grounds of Caelaelia Vasadori which is, as I said earlier, held in a time loop. Nothing filters through to your time."

"Exactly how big is that Dragon Sanctuary of his?" Hamish asked.

"About a thousand acres."

"Wow. That's impressive. So I guess the time loop was easier then, than having it exist in our time and whacking Muggle-repelling charms on it, or something."

"Yes, and besides, those charms that Harry's lot use are different to the powers that Cadeyrn uses."

"Harry's lot use?" Briana laughed. "That makes it sound like Harry Potter is a real person."

"Of course he's a real person."

Hamish dropped the rune stones he was holding in shock at that bit of news.

Briana said, "I'm sorry, but there are not a bunch of

fictional wizards and witches running around in our time."

"There might be," Hamish declared in excitement. "I mean, the whole point of their world is it exists without Muggles knowing about it, isn't it?"

"Yes, but some things that happened in the wizarding world were noticed by Muggles, like all the owls flying around when Voldemort tried to kill Harry. And bsides, if Harry Potter was real surely the 'Prime Minister' referred to throughout the series would have been 'Tony Blair' and not 'the Prime Minister'," Briana argued.

Hamish corrected her, "John Major."

"What?"

"The Harry Potter books were set between 1991 and 1997, when John Major was Prime Minister, not Tony Blair."

Briana groaned. "Whatever. Fine. Then the Prime Minister would be John Major, not 'the Prime Minister'."

"That would be true if the story had happened in your world, Lady Briana," Alasdair explained, "but it didn't."

"Where did it happen then?"

"Well, there are all sorts of realities around us, different dimensions, billions of parallel universes all stacked up against each other, and ..."

"You're quoting the Doctor, I believe," Hamish interjected.

Alasdair smiled. "As I told Briana earlier, I'll quote the truth where I find it, and the Doctor borrows many theories from Max Tegmark, William James, Hugh Everett, Stephen Hawking, and so on. But Harry Potter *is* a real person and the stories about him *are* real. However, they didn't happen on this world, they happened on a parallel one."

XIV: The Unitip

Briana couldn't' accept this. "Harry Potter is a real person living on a parallel world?" Okay, I'll admit time travel is real, and even dinosaurs are alive and well in 1513, but this? No way. This is simply too much."

Alasdair tried to explain. "You'll find a lot of the stories you humans consider fantasy or science fiction are, in fact, real stories from parallel worlds, or parallel universes, or parallel worlds in parallel universes, or even from other worlds in this universe."

Briana still didn't buy it. Hamish obviously did. "Oh, totally way past the far end of weird. So, what about the Doctor then? Is he real, too, but existing in a parallel world?"

Alasdair nodded.

"Really, really real? He really exists?"

"Indeed he does."

"Fantastic." He flashed a grin at Briana. "Those giggly friends of yours would be beside themselves if they knew the sparkly vampire actually existed somewhere. Wait, please tell me he's not real."

"Sorry, he is."

Briana shook her head. Travelling backward in time was one thing, and maybe even scientifically possible if she twisted some theorems and quantum physics around until they screamed, but what Alasdair was talking about now? No way.

Alasdair saw her shake her head. "My Lady, have you ever experienced a sense of déjà vu?"

"Yes," she replied warily.

"Well, that happens when two parallel worlds rub too close to each other. Sometimes, during déjà vu, it's even possible to slip through into another world."

"Wow, really, how?" Hamish asked.

Alasdair turned his head away from Hamish and winked at Briana. "No idea."

She suspected from Alasdair's wink that he did know how to slip into a parallel world, but that he didn't want Hamish to know he knew. Briana thought that was prudent, and changed the subject, hoping to distract Hamish.

"How did J. K. Rowling get to write Harry Potter's story? Not that I'm saying I believe you, but in theory?"

"Have you ever heard the story of how J. K. Rowling came up with the idea for the Harry Potter books?" asked Alasdair.

Briana shook her head.

Hamish, not surprisingly, knew what Alasdair was talking about. "Yeah, man. J.K. was on a train and during the trip she visualised Harry clearly walking toward her down the aisle."

He paused and frowned slightly before continuing. "She had nothing to write with, but she left the train with the whole story in her head, and I remember reading somewhere she said she was in a state of euphoria. As soon as she could, she wrote down those ideas, which subsequently became assembled into the books."

Alasdair smiled, but didn't say anything further.

Briana grasped at the edges of an idea. "So, so, you're saying that ... that sometimes fiction, is true stuff that happened on different worlds, or in different universes, that was communicated to the mind of someone who wrote the story down?"

"Yes."

"Who?" Hamish asked. "I mean, who sends the stories, and how do they send them, and how do they decide who to send them to, and are all fiction stories true?"

"Oh no, lots of them are pure fiction. You humans have some great writers with great imaginations who write great fiction. Not that I'm saying at all that those who record actual stories don't have great imaginations too, and often the real story is changed a bit, or even a lot. Artistic license and all that. And sometimes they add in fictional scenarios to the real story, which makes it even harder to tell what's real and what's not."

The gnome added another point for the twins to consider.

"But don't you find it interesting the same themes appear over and over again in your so-called fantasy writings? Elves, dragons, basilisks, phoenixes, fairies, time vortexes, unicorns, wormholes, and so on. They keep re-appearing."

Hamish frowned. "Like the blue box being bigger on the

inside, the tents at the Quidditch World Cup and Mr. Weasley's car being bigger on the inside, and Jack's bag in Liöfwende being bigger on the inside? Or like Diana Wynne Jones and Raymond Feist both writing about schools of magic long before J. K. Rowling did?"

"Exactly," Alasdair beamed. "Although such examples are more difficult to find than they should be." He laughed. "It always amuses me that most of your authors, or should I say recorders, seem to go out of their way to not mention other recorders' stories in their works, which makes their own story seem highly unlikely."

"What do you mean?" Briana asked.

"Well, for example, there are so many kids' books written after *Harry Potter*, and set in the real world, with 'real' kids as the heroes, and yet not one of the characters in those stories ever mentions *Harry Potter*. The main characters in Michael Scott's series didn't mention *Harry Potter* once, even when Josh's boss turned out to actually be Nicholas Flamel. That wouldn't happen in the real world. It's not often that you get a bunch of today's kids together for a reasonable length of time without *Harry Potter* or *Star Wars*, or something similar, being mentioned even once in the conversation." He paused. "Full marks to Russell T. and the Moff on that score."

"Who?" Briana asked, confused.

"The successive lead writers of *Doctor Who*. Their scripts always seem more viable because they do mention other stories. Like in *The Shakespeare Code* when the Doctor said 'good old J. K.' and used *Expelliarmus* to banish the Carrionites."

Briana looked blank.

"The aliens in that episode," Alasdair added by way of explanation. "They were banished using a spell from *Harry Potter*. By bringing bits from other fantasy and science fiction stories into *Doctor Who* stories, it makes their series seem so much more realistic."

Hamish argued a point. "Hang on though. If Harry Potter is real, how come when you told us about dragons you said they were Siberians and Bengals and so on? What about Chinese Fireballs, Welsh Greens, Hungarian Horntails, and Norwegian Ridgebacks? If Potter is true, wouldn't those species of dragons be the ones that existed?"

"In Potter's world, yes, and in another parallel world they have dragons called Celestials, Longwings, Regal Coppers, and Gray Widowmakers."

Hamish knew the books. "Temeraire."

"Tem-uh-what?" Briana asked.

"Tem - eh - rare. He was a Celestial Dragon who lived during the Napoleonic Wars."

"There weren't any dragons in the Napoleonic Wars."

Alasdair explained. "Not in our world, no, but in Temeraire's world, there were. Some parallel worlds are quite different to ours, some are vaguely similar, and some are almost identical except for a few points."

"Like having dragons fighting during the Napoleonic Wars," Hamish stated.

"Exactly. Or like everything being the same except Bill Nighy being the twelfth Doctor instead of Peter Capaldi."

"Oh my God, that would have been brilliant.

Glynian joined in. "I was goin' for Paterson Joseph myself. I thought they might tie him in wit' Obama somehow."

"How do you know about Obama?" Briana asked the cluricaun.

"Errr, don't most people?"

"In our time, yes, but aren't you from 1513?"

"Yes, but I use Alasdair's Riffle TV tae tune in tae your time and watch the news, documentaries, and sci-fi shows from your time."

"Oh." Briana didn't even want to think about how that worked.

Alasdair smiled at her. "Dragons are common to many worlds, but the strange thing is that while most animals that are common to many worlds, like lions, horses, and even unicorns, are the same on each world, dragons generally seem to be different on every world they exist in. Hence, you get Peruvian Vipertooths in Potter's world, Fleur-de-Nuits in Temeraire's world, and we have, or had, Siberians and Bengals.

"Anyway, back to what I was saying before. There's a planet a long way from here …"

"In a galaxy far, far way," Hamish interrupted.

Alasdair laughed. "It's called Kresimir, and it's where the Universal Historical Society is based. They're kind of like, well, an editorial office I suppose. They have Rifflecams on every planet on every world in every universe to record stories about all the different happenings and events that anyone with access to the RiffleNet can read on-line at uwrn.uhs.kr. That's the Universe Wide RiffleNet, like your World Wide Web, only much, much bigger."

"Wow, how does it work?" Hamish asked.

"Whenever data flows across the RiffleNet, the electron

movement creates resonance at the quantum level that 'echoes' across the uncollapsed probability wave functions of the various pending temporo-spatial realities. From my Riffle Room these echoes can be collected and directed to my computer."

Hamish blinked. "Ohhhh-kaaay. Whatever, fine. I'll just believe it does work, and not worry about how it actually works."

Alasdair grinned. "Good boy. The 'U-H-S' is the Universal Historical Society's domain name and the 'dot kr' is like dot com, with 'kr' being for Kresimir. Years ago a group of the UHS executives decided it would be nice if beings on technologically inferior worlds who are not connected to the RiffleNet, and who, therefore, have nothing to do with the rest of the universe, were able to gain some knowledge of the history of the universe, even if they didn't believe the stories to be true.

"So, they established a separate division within the organisation, the Unitip, whose job it was …"

"The Unitip?" Hamish interrupted.

"Oh, sorry, yes, it's an acronym. Well, it's sort of, part abbreviation, part acronym. The full name of the division is the Universal Historical Society's Technologically Inferior Planets Division, but that's a heck of a mouthful, and the acronym U.H.S.T.I.P.D. sounds a bit like 'you stupid', so instead everyone calls it the Unitip for short. It was set up to select the stories to be sent to Earth and other unconnected worlds, and to work out how to get those stories through to the humans, or other beings, who have no access to the RiffleNet. They decided the easiest way would be to select suitable humans, or other beings, on each planet and beam the ideas straight into their brains with a Riffleshot. Hamish, you're a big fan of many of the humans they selected: George Lucas, J. R. R. Tolkien, David and Leigh Eddings, Elisabeth Kay . . ."

"A few at the BBC?" Hamish interjected.

"A few at the BBC," Alasdair agreed.

"And so these people never knew that the ideas for their books or TV shows were getting beamed into their brains from a planet umpteen billion light years away?" Briana still didn't quite believe what she was hearing.

"Oh, Kresimir isn't that far away. But no, they didn't know. Well, I mean, some of them, like Jo, were more aware that the stories came from somewhere, and saw the images more clearly as a waking vision, or, as in Stephenie's case, as a dream. But obviously none of them knew exactly where the stories were coming from."

Hamish's eyes widened. "Oh my God, Alison Croggon."

Briana snickered at her brother. "That friend of yours who plays computer games with you and kicks your butt every time?"

"No, that's Alison Campbell, and she does not beat me every time," Hamish replied heatedly. "No, Alison Croggon, she wrote the awesome Books of Pellinor series. She said, on her website, that Maerad, that's the main character, appeared to her, and then Cadvan, that's the other main character, appeared, and then she started writing and the book unfolded without her thinking about it.

"She said in the end she finished the book to find out what happened, and while writing the books she was constantly amazed the world she was writing about almost seemed to be already there, and was waiting to be written down. And now I know why – the world of Edil-Amarandh and the classics of Annaren literature are true. No wonder the books seemed so real."

Briana shook her head. "I still don't know, this all seems so impossible."

"Your mum is a big fan of Richard Bach's, isn't she?" Alasdair asked Briana.

"Huge."

"Have you ever read *Jonathan Livingston Seagull?*"

"Mum read it to me when I was little."

Alasdair grinned at her. "That particular story happened on another planet, and the Unitip thought that Earth people would like the story as they had seagulls on Earth too. So, they riffleshot the story to Richard Bach. If I may quote the man himself from an interview he did with *Harper's Bazaar* in November 1972: 'It was the weirdest experience of my life. I was walking along one night, worrying about the rent money, when I heard this voice say, *"Jonathan Livingston Seagull"*. But no one was there. I had absolutely no idea what it meant. When I got home, I had a vision of a seagull flying along, and I began to write. The story certainly didn't spring from any conscious invention on my part. I just put down what I saw.'

"Unfortunately, there was a kresimirquake halfway through transmission, the equivalent of a 7.3 on your Richter Scale for earthquakes, which caused a lot of damage, including knocking out the riffleshot projector. Richard only received half the story, up to the part where Jonathan was outcast from the flock. Richard often told the story of how he had the vision for the first half of the story, but it stopped at the casting out and he had no idea how to finish it, until one day the vision of the second half of the book continued. That, of course, was when they repaired the Riffleshot projector."

Hamish added another example. "It explains Sherryl Jordan's comments too."

The reference was lost on Alasdair. "Sorry, who?".

"She's a New Zealand author. She said that she doesn't think up her ideas, that the books 'appear' to her like movies in her head, all in the space of a few seconds."

Conceding defeat to this crazy theory, Briana asked, "How do we know which stories are true and which aren't?"

"Ah, well," Alasdair sighed, "that's the problem, see, they never thought that one through. I guess it's a little like you really have no way of knowing what's true on the internet, and what isn't. There's a record at the Unitip of the stories that have been riffleshot out, and if I put my hand on a book while clasping my necklace I can tell whether it's true or not, but humans themselves have no way of telling. Anyway, enough for one day, I can see your brain is starting to fry. What say we have a nice cup of tea?"

Glynian let out a whoop.

Alasdair looked at him in surprise. "Aren't you more a Lagavulin man?"

"Oh I dinnae want a cup o' tea laddie, bloody dishwater, but maybe a Lagavulin to celebrate is a good idea, aye." He had beaten Hamish in their backgammon game. Hamish closed the board in annoyance at losing to the cluricaun.

"Dude, you said Llewellyn gave the Atlas to that dragon

keeper, but I presume Llewellyn took it back after he killed him. How did you get it to give to Briana?"

Alasdair's expression became sombre as he remembered the murder of Gryffydd. "I was spying on Cadeyrn when he killed Gryffydd. Cadeyrn doesn't look after the castle well, and the mortar is crumbling in many places. If you know where to look, which I do, you can look into many rooms in the castle from those next door, or above. I knew where he kept the Atlas and, using my powers, I made it past the guards, took the book, and escaped here, to my Riffle Room, where I've kept it safe since then. Well, almost. It's been back in the world since you were born."

"Where?"

"In Abergavenny."

"Who was looking after it?" Hamish asked

Alasdair blushed a little. "Oh, umm, people in Abergavenny."

"What …"

Briana knew Alasdair well enough to know he wouldn't answer that question so she cut Hamish off, asking instead, "Why did you give the Atlas to me?"

"I have my reasons."

"Care to share those reasons?"

Alasdair didn't say anything.

Hamish tried again. "You are one exasperating bloody gnome. Why can't you tell us? Seriously Alasdair, after everything else you've said, and everything we've experienced, nothing would surprise us anymore."

Alasdair remained silent.

"Grrrrrr," Hamish growled, before turning away in

disgust, and opening the backgammon board again.

"Best of three?" he asked Glynian.

Briana hoped Alasdair would answer some of the things that puzzled her.

"You mentioned earlier that Cadeyrn wants to take over the world and keep it as it was in medieval times. But wouldn't that mean that he'd be living in the same state as everyone else? I mean, it's not like he'd have TV or radio or electricity or anything like that, because they wouldn't exist anymore."

"Cadeyrn knows, and would still know, of the possibility of your current future, even if he destroys the path to it from the past. If he takes over the world in the seventh century, and those effects ripple through to your current time so that in your new time everyone will live in a medieval state, he will still be able to access the possibility of your current time, using his necklace, and will be able to bring anything from your old possible time continuum into your new actual time continuum.

"He will be able to have electricity, phones, television, radio, the internet and so on in his castle. To the people of your new medieval present it will seem like everything he has is magic and he is a God, especially as he's Immortal."

"But, if our time becomes medieval how would, say, a television work? Where would the broadcasts come from?" Briana asked. "There wouldn't be any TV programs any-more, would there?"

"A television of Cadeyrn's could pick up the discontinued broadcast frequencies from the universe's memories of the possibility of your time continuum as it is known to you.

Your modern time would be replaced by Cadeyrn's medieval time, but as your modern time would have already existed, even if it no longer existed, the memory of it would still be there in the universe and Cadeyrn could tune in to that."

Briana's eyes widened.

Alasdair smiled. "Your world would be in a state of medieval existence, but Cadeyrn could still sit at night and watch *Supernatural* on TV. You don't need to know how it works, just know that it does work so you are aware of the danger of what Cadeyrn can do. He's spent centuries waiting for technology to reach its heights of today."

Briana interrupted Alasdair. "Why has he waited so long then? I mean, couldn't he have travelled to our time from his time and get what he needed and take it back to his own time? Why wait for the time to happen?"

"Time travel is only possible into the past, or into a future that has already happened. To travel forward in time, you must have first travelled back in time, and you cannot travel forward in time further than your own present. The past has happened and is fixed, or rather semi-fixed; the future has infinite possibilities, depending on the choices that are made in the present, and until they happen, it is not possible to travel to the one that will happen, because you don't know which possibility will happen until it does. The obvious exception to the rule, as Hamish pointed out earlier, are, or were, the Time Lords."

Hamish made a move against Glynian, but was still obviously following the conversation. "How are you planning on stopping him?"

Glynian was concentrating on the board "It's nae him

that's gonna stop Llewellyn, it's you, you and yer sister."

"Glynian!"

"Us?" The twins looked at each other. Briana managed to speak before Hamish. "What good will we be against someone who's been building his powers for hundreds of years?" She saw Alasdair aim a sharp glance at Glynian, which made the cluricaun blush.

Alasdair attempted to brush off her concern. "I'll explain it to you once you've developed your powers more. It's nothing you should worry about for now."

Briana was about to point out the insanity of telling them they had to save the world, but not to worry about it for now, when Alasdair continued.

"I'm here to guide you and to teach you, and there are certain things I won't tell you until a little later, no, Hamish, don't ask me to. There is no need to worry before you're ready. I have every confidence in you. For now I have things to do in another part of time and you need to return to your own time to solve the next riddle in the Atlas."

Briana started to say, "We'd worry less if ..."

"No."

Hamish tried, "But we ..."

"No."

Hamish sighed.

Briana also wanted to ask Alasdair more about how she and Hamish were supposed to stop an invincible, immortal, time-traveling knight from taking over the world, but knew that Alasdair wouldn't tell them. Of course she'd worry, who wouldn't? She looked over at Hamish. The look on his face told her that at least she wouldn't have to worry alone.

Hamish also obviously knew the futility of trying to get anything more out of Alasdair, because his next question was, "What are you guys going to do after Bree and I go back to Abergavenny?"

"Good question. Glynian, what do you want to do? Return to your own time, or stay with me?"

Glynian considered the options. "Well, I dinnae think there's anythin' for me back in 1513 right noo. Wi' McDonal' takin' o'er the castle I would no' like to be there anymore. I'll come wi' you, Alasdair."

"Good, you can help me with some things I need to do." He looked at the twins. "You two should get going."

"What? No, I'm in the middle of a game here."

Alasdair sighed in resignation. "Lady Briana, shall we collect Rashid while we wait?"

Strolling with Alasdair to the shore of the pool, Briana could see Kenai cruising the lake with Rashid riding on his back, clinging to the whale's dorsal fin. Briana had been so engrossed in the conversation that she hadn't noticed Rashid wake up and join the killer whale. She called out to them. Kenai sloshed to a stop at the edge of the lake, and Rashid jumped off and scampered into Briana's arms.

"Hey Mum, that was sooooo much fun, Kenai rocks."

Sitting on the shore, Briana chatted with Alasdair, Rashid, and Kenai until Hamish and Glynian finally joined them. (Glynian had won again, to Hamish's obvious annoyance.)

Alasdair gave them instructions to get them back to Tyn-y-Bryn. "Briana, Hamish, hold hands, take Kenai's fin, and Rashid's paw, and Briana can riffle you to your own time. Kenai and Rashid will be toyed once you get back there."

"No way, dude," Kenai cried, diving under the surface in a movement that splashed them all, and reappearing at the far end of the lake. "I am A-LIVE, man," he shouted back to them. "I ain't going back to being no one's soft toy. I'm real, and I'm staying here. Come visit some time, dudes."

Briana looked at Alasdair. "Is that okay? Can Kenai stay here?"

"Or will it upset the quantum jiggery-pokery thingummies with the wibbly-wobbly bits?" Hamish asked.

Alasdair laughed. "No, Hamish, it'll be fine. However …"

He clasped his necklace, gestured, and with a few words set the lake so that the supply of fish wouldn't run out, no matter how much Kenai ate.

Kenai was overjoyed when Alasdair explained what he had done. "Coooool, thanks man." Diving again, he soon re-surfaced in front of the group, sending a misty spray of water over Briana, before turning and drenching Hamish by way of farewell. Briana dried her brother off.

Briana did her best to give Kenai a farewell hug, but had to settle for a pat.

"I love you, Mum," he cried, before taking another great dive and disappearing.

Briana looked at Rashid. "What about you? Do you want to stay here too?" Rashid jumped up into her arms and threw his paws around her neck.

"Well, it's fun being alive, but I am really, really tired, and I guess being a toy again will be as good as a kip. And you'll be heading off after you've solved the next riddle, so I won't be toyed for long, will I? I'll come back with you for now."

"That's settled then. We'd better all get moving."

Glynian gave Briana an enormous hug, and shook hands with Hamish. "Take care, lassie, and you too, laddie. And hone yer skills. I dinnae want tae be gettin' bored wi' beatin' you at backgammon."

Hamish narrowed his eyes at the cluricaun, who laughed.

"How do we get back to Abergavenny?" Briana asked Alasdair.

"Clasp your necklace, picture your room in Abergavenny in your head, and say '*Riffle in*,'" Alasdair told her.

Linking her left arm with Hamish and using her left hand to hold her necklace, Briana held Rashid in place on her right hip, and pictured their bedroom in Abergavenny in her mind. "*Riffle in*." The three of them dissolved instantly into green tunnels, making Briana aware of the natural talent she had for using the Atlas.

Once they phphted out into their bedroom at Tyn-y-Bryn, Rashid cried excitedly, "I'm still real, Mum. We're back in our own time, and I'm still alive. I'm a real monkey. How wonderful."

Hamish voiced what Briana was thinking. "I am sooooo glad we didn't bring Kenai back with us."

XV: A Knowledge of Guinevere

Briana laughed, hugged Rashid, and with great under-statement said, "That could have presented us with a small problem. Oh, how wonderful you're still alive."

She was surprised to see Aunty Alys's dog, Busby, in their room, until she remembered that, to their 'present time', events were just as they had left them.

The disturbance with Cadeyrn entering their bedroom had only happened fifteen minutes before they left. It was still only 3.30 on Thursday morning, and Briana could hear the murmur of the adults' voices from downstairs. It was strange to return and find no time had passed after going through so much.

Hamish pointed at Rashid. "What are we going to do about that?"

"I don't know, we'll …" Briana stopped at the sound of a crash from downstairs. "Oh, no, Hamish, Cadeyrn's followed us here!"

"Calm down, Bree, he's dead in 655 for a week, remember?" Hamish walked out the door.

"Rashid, stay here," Briana told the monkey.

"Not fair. I wanna come down, I wanna see what's happening, I wanna …"

"Hush, Rashid. Please wait here for now, I'll be back soon. You'll have to stay here until we can figure out how to explain you." She shut the door behind her and left Rashid in the room.

Uncle Wynn called to them from the bottom of the stairs, and pointed at the slate floor. "Careful kids." A cup and saucer lay shattered in a puddle of tea.

"What happened?" Briana asked.

Dad wouldn't meet Briana's eyes. "I accidentally knocked a tea cup off the table. It's nothing to worry about, go on back to bed."

Briana looked anxiously at Mum, who was sitting at the table and looked awfully pale, then reluctantly followed Hamish to their room. Soon she heard the murmur of their parents' voices in the bedroom next door, followed by footsteps heading back downstairs.

Hamish looked at this sister. "They're talking garbage. Let's go listen in and see if we can find out what's going on. I'm sure Dad didn't knock that tea cup, Mum dropped it."

"I don't like spying on them."

"How else will we find out what's happening? They won't tell us anything, they forget we're not five anymore." He left and Briana, who agreed he had a point, followed, once again asking Rashid to stay in the room.

From the corridor Briana could hear the low voices of the adults around the dining table, and from the top of the stairs she could make out Aunty Aly's words.

"How long has this been going on, and what symptoms are we talking about?

The question was obviously directed at Dad, as it was his voice she heard replying. "It's been happening for a while now. At least we've managed to mostly keep it hidden from the kids."

Hamish nudged Briana. "See."

Dad continued. "She's been drowsy and lethargic, but she hates the heat and it's summer at home right now, so we put it down to that. She was getting headaches for a bit, and was nauseous in the mornings. At first we thought she might be pregnant," (the twins looked at each other), "but that was negative, and the nausea stopped anyway, so again, we thought it must be something to do with the weather. She's also been having problems with her memory, but we put that down to stress at school with the new principal.

"She made an appointment to see Trish a few times. That's her doctor and she won't trust anyone except Trish, but she's often booked full so Isabel had to book a week in advance. Then, when the appointment came due her symptoms had gone, so she cancelled. And because her symptoms came and went, we kept putting everything down to stress or the weather." He paused, before continuing in a broken voice.

"But now she's collapsed I'm worried it's something serious after all, and I wish she had gone to see Trish, even if she didn't have any symptoms at the time she went."

Aunty Alys's voice sounded soothing. "Well, she's sleeping now so we'll leave her till morning, then we'll run her to the hospital for a few tests." The sound of chairs being pushed back sent the twins racing back to their room and jumping into their beds. Rashid was sitting on the end of Briana's bed.

She heard a squeak of the floorboard outside their room. "I'll just check on the kids."

Hamish looked at the monkey. "Oh no, Rashid, quick, get under the bed."

Too late. The door opened and Dad came in.

"Hello, you two, still got the light on? Come on now, it's very late, or, rather, very early. Time to sleep." He picked up the toy monkey from the end of the bed and tucked it in with Briana. He kissed her forehead and tweaked Rashid's nose. Hamish dived under his covers.

"Don't even think of kissing me, old man."

Dad smiled, winked at Briana, and kissed the covers over Hamish. "Goodnight, sleep well."

"You too, Dad," Briana replied.

As their father left, Rashid once again untoyed and came alive.

Hamish looked at him quizzically. "Wow, that was a neat trick. How'd you do it?"

Rashid didn't know, and neither did Briana, but it was certainly a relief. It would have been difficult explaining the presence of a real monkey in their bedroom.

After talking quietly for a while about all they'd been through, Hamish poked his head out the door to listen. "All clear. Come on, Bree, I want to check something,"

The three of them sneaked down the stairs and into the study. Hamish closed the door behind them, and Briana watched as he turned the computer on and went onto

Google. With Briana's help in remembering what Dad had said, he typed Mum's symptoms in and hit search.

Hamish grumbled about the speed on the dial-up connection as they waited. When the results eventually appeared, Briana felt sick. The first site was titled 'Brain Tumour Symptoms' and the second was 'Cancer Symptoms'.

"Oh Hamish, Mum can't have brain cancer, that's too horrible to even consider."

Hamish cautioned her, "Hold your horses Bree, there are lots of other things it could be. You heard Dad; they even thought Mum might be pregnant at one point."

"But she wasn't."

"Well, no, but it could be something else. Let's not get too upset by guesses yet."

"What if we've guessed right?"

"Our guesses could easily be wrong."

"What if they're not?"

"Then we'll see. And don't 'what if' me like that, you sound like Garion."

"Who's Garion?"

"Never mind. Come on, we'd better get back to bed before the olds catch us here."

When Briana woke several hours later, Hamish was reading something on his Kindle, no doubt a fantasy novel.

"Morning," she greeted him, and received a grunt in reply. She looked at the Kindle. This was the first time she had thought of one of Hamish's books as a 'fantasy novel' and not a 'stupid fantasy novel'. She'd never call his books stupid again, because half of them would probably turn out to be no more fictional than her science books were. Crazy.

Hamish misinterpreted Briana's stare. "Look, Bree, I'm sure everything will be fine, it's probably recurring bouts of the flu, or something."

"It's that 'or something' that worries me."

"Well, I'm going for breakfast, see you there."

After he left, Briana climbed out of bed, dressed, and put her make-up on.

"Rashid, you should stay here."

"I want to come with you."

"But you turn into a toy around anyone except us."

"I don't care."

"All right, come on then." Settling Rashid on her hip she headed down the stairs, and found Hamish sitting at the dining room table. She could hear Aunty Alys moving around in the kitchen.

Hamish choked on a mouthful of cereal. "Oh crap, Bree."

"What?"

Hamish pointed at Rashid, who hadn't toyed even though they could see Aunty Alys.

"Quick, take him back to our room."

Before Briana could move she heard Aunty Alys murmur something from the kitchen. Briana started in surprise as Rashid was toyed.

Hamish looked toward the kitchen. "Did she just … ?"

Briana shrugged, and called to their Aunt, "Good morning. Did you say something?"

"Just singing, dear."

Briana raised one eyebrow, noting Hamish also looked sceptical.

"Where are Mum and Dad?" Briana asked.

Aunty Alys kept her back to the twins. "Oh, they've, um, gone into town early to, ah, do some shopping."

"Yeah, right," Hamish mouthed to Briana.

"Do you want anything special for Waitangi Day?" Aunty Alys asked the twins.

"What?" Hamish asked.

Briana looked at her watch. "Oh gosh, it's the fifth of February. I can't believe I forgot it's Waitangi Day tomorrow."

"Easy enough to do when crossing time zones," Aunty Alys assured her.

Briana drew in a sharp breath, but it was Hamish who asked the question. "What time zones?"

"The international date line of course. And you're on holiday, so it's easy enough to lose track of the days."

"Oh, right, yeah."

Waitangi Day was a public Holiday in New Zealand commemorating the signing of the Treaty of Waitangi, New Zealand's founding document, in 1840. As far back as Briana could remember, she and Hamish had joined their parents at the dawn service on the summit of Mauao until 2010. The event was cancelled in 2011 due to slips on the mountain, and then moved to the smaller, but more accessible, Hopukiore.

Briana and Hamish told their Aunt they weren't expecting anything. Waitangi Day was not a gift-giving day.

She winked at them. "Well, we may make an exception tomorrow. Now, after breakfast how would you like to go for a horse ride? I'm sure the two of you would like to get away for a bit by yourselves." Her deceptively mild tone somehow suggested any arguments would be useless. "I have to go and help Wynn in the cottage. I'll send him to get the saddles down for you."

"Ah, Aunty Alys, we can't ride," Briana told her.

"What?"

"We can't ride horses."

"You live on a farm," her Aunt pointed out.

"A free-range chicken farm; we don't have horses. The last time I was on a 'horse' was when Mum took us to the Shetland pony track when we were about eight." She stopped, and grinned.

"The time Hamish's pony stopped dead in front of a thorn bush and flipped him into – ow."

"Don't hit your sister, Hamish. I'm sure you can ride just fine." There was a glint in her eye. "It's not that hard. Make sure you're home in time for lunch. Now, I should get to the cottage. Enjoy yourselves." She left the house, with the dogs, Rosy and Busby, at her heels, muttering something as she disappeared from sight. Rashid untoyed.

Hamish stared at Rashid. "She knows."

"Knows what?"

"She knows about Rashid. She said something before that toyed him, a spell or something, and then she untoyed him."

"Hamish, that's impossible."

"Oh for goodness sake Briana, we spent last night in Scotland in 1513, Rashid and Kenai became real, and we found out that Harry Potter and the Doctor are real, so 'impossible' is kind of the name of the game right now. It wouldn't surprise me to discover that Aunty Alys is an alien princess from another planet hiding on Earth."

"Oh, Hamish, my brain is fried enough right now without

Aunty Alys being from, from, Mars or something. It's all too unreal."

"You did believe everything Alasdair said, didn't you?" Hamish asked.

"Hamish, I don't know what to believe any more. Look, I believe in science, I'm top of physics, and biology, and chemistry, and I ... oh, Rashid just toyed again." Briana saw Uncle Wynn walking toward them from the cottage, talking to himself.

"Hello, you two. Your aunt tells me you're off for a ride. Come on then, I'll help you lift the saddles down, they're a bit heavy."

"But Uncle Wynn, we don't – ow," Briana exclaimed, as Hamish stood on her foot.

Hamish looked at her and shook his head slightly. "Let's just roll with this and see what happens," he whispered.

"Fine," she whispered back, "but stop hitting me and standing on me. I'll be covered in bruises at this rate."

In the stable their uncle took a set of keys out of his pocket and undid the padlocks holding the saddles and bridles in place on the wall.

"A sad sign of the times. We lost two saddles last year. Now then, this is Lancelot," he placed a saddle next to the black horse, and indicated that Hamish should ride him, "and this is Guinevere." He placed another saddle next to the beautiful grey mare. "Have fun. I'd better get back to the cottage; that ceiling won't paint itself."

Leaving them standing there, he headed back towards the cottage, and Briana heard him mutter something under his breath. Rashid untoyed again and gushed, "Horses, wow, how exciting, are we going riding, are we gonna go racing over the hills on them, how cool, can I ride the black one?"

"Sorry, mate, you're going with her."

"He's not going with anyone, Hamish. We don't even know how to put on the saddles, much less ride, and … what are you doing?" Hamish had gone over to a bench, taken a soft brush, and was in the process of brushing Lancelot.

"I'm making sure that no twigs or burrs will become lodged underneath the saddle pad while we're out."

"How do you know to do that?"

"No idea," he replied with a grin. He finished brushing Lancelot, and then placed a saddle pad across the horse's back.

"Make sure it covers the withers," Briana told him.

Hamish laughed. "And how would you know to tell me that?"

Briana's eyes widened. "I don't know, I just, I … I just knew, but I don't know, but I, oh man. I hoped nothing weird would happen today."

Hamish laughed again. Briana glared at him, then brushed Guinevere down, and put on the saddle pad (watching the withers) and the saddle, making sure there were no places where the saddle was touching the horse's skin and that the saddle flaps were all lying flat.

After wrapping the girth around the horse's chest and girthing to the first hole, she dropped the stirrup irons and checked for the correct length by placing her fingers at the top of the stirrup leathers and placing the stirrup irons by her underarm, adjusting the length to suit. She took the bridle and pulled it over Guinevere's head, making sure her ears didn't get pinned underneath, and let Guinevere take the bit.

Next, she placed the chinstrap across Guinevere's throat, making sure the horse had plenty of room to breathe, and checked to make sure the bit was in the proper place. Once she had finished, she looked at Hamish.

"Right, let's tighten these girths and get out there." He led Lancelot out of the stable.

Briana looked at Rashid who commented, "That's cool, Mum, I didn't know you knew how to saddle a horse. Where did you learn that?"

"I didn't. I've never done it before. Rashid, my sole experience of fully grown horses has been to pat them on the muzzles at the Mystery Creek Fieldays, and yet as I brushed Guinevere it was like I knew exactly what to do, as if I had done this a thousand times before."

"Hurry up Briana," Hamish called from outside.

Briana led Guinevere outside, with Rashid following, and found Hamish was already sitting on Lancelot. "See you at the top of the hill. Hah!"

Briana put her foot in the stirrup and swung onto Guinevere's back. A few weeks back, she and her friend Roanna had hired pushbikes at the Mount and gone for a ride along Marine Parade and Oceanbeach Road. Briana hadn't been on a bike for a couple of years before that, but when she got on the bike that Sunday it was as if she had been biking only the day before. Swinging onto Guinevere felt the same; like she had ridden horses all her life. Rashid leapt onto Guinevere's tail and climbed up, sitting in front of Briana.

"Hold on to the saddle," she told him, before nudging Guinevere into a walk, a trot, and a gallop.

Tyn-y-Bryn is Welsh for 'Home on the Hill', and Abergavenny is nestled in the valley of seven hills. The house itself was located halfway up the Sugarloaf Mountain. After galloping up the hill Briana found Hamish waiting for her at the top, his face flushed with excitement. "Wicked, man, that was fantastic. I had no idea riding a horse would be such brilliant fun."

"Hamish, how the hell did we saddle the horses like we've done it all our lives and ride the horses like we've done it all our lives? It's impossible."

Hamish looked pointedly at Rashid. "Change the damn record, Bree. Your toys are alive, we've been traveling through time, Harry Potter is real, and you're worried because you can ride a horse? Chillax and enjoy it. Hah!" He rode off again.

"Well," Briana grumbled to Rashid, "I am enjoying it, I'm just wondering how I know how to do it." She took off after Hamish. They spent a couple of hours racing across the Welsh countryside on Lancelot and Guinevere, before heading back to Tyn-y-Bryn for lunch.

As they approached the house Briana saw their rental car. "Oh look, Mum and Dad are back. Come on." The twins unsaddled the horses and put them back in the paddock before rushing inside, not even stopping to play with the puppies.

Dad, Aunty Alys, and Uncle Wynn were sitting at the table drinking cups of tea. Aunty Alys was holding Dad's hand, and she had red eyes.

"Where's Mum?" Briana asked in a quiet voice, holding the newly toyed Rashid close to her chest.

Dad's voice sounded strained when he replied, "She stayed in town to do some more shopping."

Briana gave her father a stern look. "We're not that stupid, Dad. Tell us what's wrong."

He sighed. "All right. Actually, she's in the hospital. They're running a few tests to find out why she's a little off-colour." He tried to smile. "But don't worry. I'm sure it's nothing serious."

Briana burst into tears and threw herself into her father's arms. "Oh Dad," she sobbed, "Mum's got brain cancer, hasn't she?".

XVI: The Town of Many Colours

B riana," Hamish hissed.

Dad looked at him. "Hamish? Why does Briana think your mother has brain cancer?"

"Because she's a drama queen?"

"Hamish." Dad's tone was familiar to the twins.

Hamish knew he couldn't fool his father. "We, ahh, overheard you talking last night. I put all the symptoms you mentioned Mum had into Google and it took us to a website that told us she probably has brain cancer."

"Oh Hamish, don't go borrowing trouble, you can't rely on Google for an accurate diagnosis of symptoms. Remember that time your friend Lachlan tried to diagnose his stomach bug on-line and was told he was most likely pregnant? Let's wait and see what the doctor says."

He shut off any further debate by adding, "Now, your aunt has made a great lunch for us, so we should all eat something and not worry too much yet."

Briana managed a small smile. "Okay," she agreed,

although she knew she'd still worry in private.

Lunch was a mostly sad affair. The adults and Briana picked at their food, but nothing curbed Hamish's appetite. Taking four slices of freshly-baked bread he smothered them all in butter, piled chicken on the first slice, bacon on the second, and tomato, lettuce, and cheese on the third. He covered the chicken in pesto, the bacon in avocado, put the entire thing together as one huge sandwich, managed to take a bite of the entire thing at once, stopped eating, looked at Briana, jumped up from the table without excusing himself, and raced upstairs.

"Hamish?" Dad called.

"I'll go and see what's wrong, excuse me." Briana gathered the toy Rashid and ran up the stairs to their room, where Rashid untoyed and jumped onto her bed.

Hamish was sitting on his bed with his translations from the Atlas in front of him. He beckoned excitedly to Briana as she came in, stabbing his finger on the page, and cut through Rashid's chatter. "Look, Bree, the Atlas, the Elixir."

"What about it?"

He read from the translation. "'The Key to Immortality for the Healthy, the Key to Life for the Terminal.' Don't you see? If Mum does have brain cancer, and if it's terminal, we can save her, the Elixir will save her. 'The Key to Life for the Terminal', what else could that mean? If the Atlas can take us to different places and times, and make Kenai and Rashid real, and Alasdair live forever, I'm sure it could cure Mum's cancer too, if that's what she has. So, let's see if we can crack the next riddle and get on with the Quest."

Briana, much to Hamish' annoyance, had locked the Atlas in her suitcase as she struggled to process what they'd been through. Now she unlocked her suitcase, took the Atlas out, and turned to the page after the riddle about Loch Ness.

The next set of runes was waiting for them. Briana looked at Hamish. "All right then, go for it."

He grinned at her, took a pen and paper from his bedside table, and translated the riddle. After reading it to Briana he looked thoughtful. "Well, I'm guessing a ship sunk by 'something quite cold and white' is the *Titanic*, that was sunk by an iceberg. We're going to the *Titanic*? Fantastic."

Briana shook her head and pointed to his translation. "No, look, there's a town the ship stopped at before she sank, a 'town of many colours'. We need to find out where the *Titanic* stopped and go there."

Hamish looked at her. "Google." Closing the Atlas, he handed it to Briana, who put it back in her suitcase. "Rashid, do you want to come with us or stay here? You'll be toyed if we go downstairs," she told him.

"In that case I might stay here. I mean, I don't mind the being toyed itself, it's like having a kip, but the actual toying and untoying does leave me with a bit of a headache."

Briana looked concerned, "Really? I didn't know that."

"Can you bring me back something to eat? Bananas?"

"Bananas. Bananas are good," Hamish said.

"What?"

"Never mind. Glynian would get it."

"Whatever. *Bananas.*" Holding her necklace, she produced three large bananas for Rashid.

"Oh, cool, thanks Mum, I forgot you can do that."

Smiling at the monkey, Briana left the room and headed downstairs, followed by Hamish, and found the adults were still at the dining table. They looked up as the twins appeared. "Are you two okay?" Dad asked.

"Fine," Hamish replied. "I, uhh, had something in my eye. Briana helped me get it out. Aunty Alys, can we use your computer? We need to e-mail some friends."

"Of course, but don't you want to finish your lunch first?" She gestured at the almost untouched sandwich.

"Oh, yeah," Hamish began, but stopped as Briana stood on his foot. He looked at her and whispered, "Yeah, like that's not going to look suspicious."

Briana fumed in frustration while she waited for him to finish eating, too worried to eat anything herself.

There was another long wait for the old computer to get going, after which Hamish typed 'Titanic' into Google and had close to a hundred million hits.

"You need to narrow that down a little."

"Thanks Brains, I never would have guessed."

Briana ignored that.

A search for 'Titanic Itinerary' cut the hits to under four hundred thousand, and Hamish soon managed to find the name of the last port of call. "Aha, here we go, Cob, Cob, ummm, Cob-huh. How's it pronounced?"

"I don't know, but type it in and see what comes up."

Hamish typed 'Cobh' and hit search.

"Ah, here we go. It's pronounced "Cove'," he read from the Wikipedia page. "'Cobh, known from 1850 until 1920 as Queenstown, is a tourist seaport town on the south coast of County Cork, Ireland.' And let me zoom in on that picture, aha, look at the houses all painted different colours. The riddle said 'in this town of many colours', this has to be it."

"That looks impressive." Briana pointed at a magnificent gothic-medieval looking building.

Hamish read the caption. "St. Colman's Cathedral." He skimmed through the rest of the page, and then tried a few other sites, but couldn't find anything about mythical beasts that were supposed to be living in caves nearby.

He discovered Cobh was the largest island in Cork Harbour. Reading over his shoulder, Briana was surprised that around two and a half million immigrants had left Ireland from the port between 1848 and 1950, the equivalent of half the population of New Zealand leaving.

Muttering again about the speed, or lack of, of the dial-up connection, Hamish eventually gave up. Shutting the computer down, the twins headed back to their room, telling Aunty Alys they were going to have an afternoon nap. Uncle Wynn had gone back to work on the cottage, and Dad had gone to help him. Once upstairs, the twins closed the door.

Hamish looked thoughtful. "Do we need the name of the beasts?"

"We did last time."

"Maybe we didn't. Yes, I said 'Loch Ness Monster', but maybe 'Loch Ness' was the trigger rather than 'monster'. It is an atlas, after all, so we might as well give it a try."

"Okay, but we should go a little better prepared this time, in case we arrive in the middle of winter or something."

"Good idea," Hamish agreed. He looked at Briana's long pink floral skirt and lacy long-sleeved white shirt. "And if we have to run away from anything nasty, you're not exactly dressed for it."

"What should I wear?"

Hamish flipped her suitcase open. "Well, nothing in there. Don't you own anything except girly clothes?"

"Do you mind?"

"Not at all. I know, hang on a minute." He took his cell phone out of his pocket, tapped a few keys, and showed a picture to Briana. "There you are, ideal. Wear that."

"You have got to be kidding." The picture showed a woman with long black hair wearing black leather pants and a black leather vest with a bare midriff. "Who is that?"

"Aeryn Sun."

"Who?"

"Never mind. What's wrong with it?"

"What's ... no."

"Fine." He tapped his phone a few times. "How about this?"

Briana looked at the picture: a woman with shoulder-length brown hair wearing a pair of khaki pants, an olive green singlet top, and a khaki jacket.

"Hamish, I am not dressing as Helen Cutter."

"Fine, sort yourself out then. Turn around, I'm changing the normal way."

Briana turned her back on Hamish, clasped her necklace, and dressed herself in a pair of plain blue jeans, a plain white T-shirt, and a plain black sweatshirt. When she turned back she found Hamish was wearing his black Fetid Cat Drool jeans, a *Doctor Who* T-shirt, a *Stargate* military jacket, and his Shark Alley joggers. He put some extra sweatshirts and wet weather gear for them both into a *Star Trek* backpack, the one with the large *Legend of the Seeker* patch sewn on it, and put his *Farscape* baseball cap on. "Okay, let's go."

Briana laughed at him. "For someone who says he doesn't follow fashion, you're a walking ad for merchandise."

Briana sat Rashid on her lap, took Hamish's hand with her left hand, and with her right hand she touched the little red dragon symbol at the bottom of the riddle page. "Cobh."

As with the riddle about Loch Ness, this caused a map to form on the right-hand page, this time of southern Ireland.

"Sweet, it's working," Hamish stated the obvious.

Once the map of Ireland filled in, Briana took her finger off the little red dragon symbol, which moved to the south coast. Once it had settled, she touched the red dragon again, and the three of them dissolved into individual tunnels of green stars.

As she was phphted out of her tunnel Briana heard a 'splash', followed by indignant cries from Rashid and hysterical laughter from Hamish.

"Muuuuum," Rashid cried, climbing out of a toilet bowl, "Mum, how disgusting, I'm soaked, that wasn't funny, how could you do that to me, shut up Hamish, why did you pick a toilet, shut up Hamish, couldn't you have landed us on a nice park bench or something, shut up Hamish, or in a toy shop or at a restaurant, or – SHUT UP HAMISH!"

"I'm – I'm – I'm sorry," Hamish attempted to stop laughing, and failed.

Briana helped Rashid out and dried him off with a word and a gesture. She looked around. They had, indeed, phphted out in a restroom. It was a large cylindrical room with a toilet, basin, hand dryer, and mirror. There was a handle saying 'Push down to open', which Hamish did. The twins stepped outside onto a street filled with people. Rashid was instantly toyed, cutting off his complaints.

They found themselves by the Cobh Heritage Centre.

Hamish pointed to the cars. "They look fairly modern, and the tunnel was green. I don't think we've moved in time." A poster for *The Irish Times* on a daily street billboard confirmed that it was 'today', and when Briana asked someone what the time was, the answer agreed with the time on her watch; just after one in the afternoon. Hamish looked disappointed.

Briana walked over to a bronze statue, and read the plaque. When Hamish joined her she told him, "It's a memorial to those who died when the *Lusitania* was sunk off the coast in 1915." Above the town they could see the majestic spires of the cathedral and decided to head there.

They walked along Lower Road until it joined Westbourne Place, turned left at a street called Pearse Square, right onto Rahilly Street, and then left onto Cathedral Place. Briana laughed when she looked back towards the town. The houses, which from the front were so colourful, were plain concrete on the back. "It's like they're on a movie set."

Briana was awestruck by St. Colman's Cathedral, and Hamish exclaimed, "Fantastic, there's nothing like this at home. Man, you could hold a wicked sci-fi convention in there."

The outside of the building showed minute attention to detail, and inside it was even more impressive, pure Gothic grandeur. Briana stared up, and up, and up at the massive marble pillars, the stained glass windows, the beautiful arches, and the carvings of Irish saints and famous churchmen.

Looking into the cathedral she could see a large pulpit off to the right, an intricately carved work of Austrian oak according to Hamish, who was reading off a flyer he had found at the entrance.

"Come on Bree, we'll be able to take a great photo from there." Hamish walked over and unclipped the velvet rope across the bottom of the staircase. He took his phone out of the back pocket of his jeans.

Briana didn't want to follow him, and glanced nervously over at the other people looking through the Cathedral. "It's probably cordoned off for a reason."

"Oh come on ya wuss, it won't bite."

Looking around to make sure no one was watching them, Briana followed Hamish onto the staircase. There was an explosion of red smoke and flashes of lightning, and Briana's whole body was thrown violently to the side. She found herself flying through a tunnel of blue stars, before being phphted out to land in a heap on a floor.

Looking around she saw they were now in a small room, and Rashid had untoyed again. Two bunk beds stood against one wall, and a little table and washbasin were positioned under a porthole. Briana peered out and could see water moving past. Not a small room then, a small cabin. On a ship.

"Briana, what the hell did you do?" Hamish demanded.

"Me? I ... nothing, well, nothing consciously that is. I don't know what happened."

"Where are we?"

"How would I know? I didn't do anything. Maybe you did it."

"Me? I didn't do anything."

"Well, let's see where we are." Briana opened the door.

Out in the corridor (where Rashid toyed), they received strange looks from the people they met. Everyone else seemed to be dressed in olden-style clothes similar to what Briana and Hamish had worn in their final year at primary school when their class had dressed up for a school trip to the gold mine in Waihi.

"Maybe you should change our clothes into something more, umm, suitable," Hamish suggested. They returned to the cabin and Briana swapped their clothes for ones similar to what the people in the corridor wore.

"Hamish, do you think we're where I think we are?"

"That'd be my guess. The riddle talked about the *Titanic*, we're obviously in a ship's cabin, and the clothes those people are wearing look about right for 1912."

"But how did we get here?"

"I don't know, but if we are on the *Titanic*, it does not bode well for our longevity." Hamish headed back into the corridor.

They found their way to an open deck, where the iconic funnels overhead confirmed exactly what ship they were on, and a newspaper lying on a deckchair said it was Thursday the eleventh of April, 1912.

Hamish glanced at the newspaper, "Three days."

"What?"

"The *Titanic* sank on the fourteenth of April, in three days' time."

Briana gasped. "Oh my God. Hamish, we have to stop it."

"Stop what?"

"Stop the ship from sinking. Most of these people are going to drown, we have to stop it, we have to warn them." Briana looked around for someone in authority, but Hamish stepped in front of her and took hold of both her arms.

"We can't, Bree. Look, first, no one would believe us, they all consider her 'unsinkable', second, they're not going to believe we're from the future, and third, remember what Alasdair said? We can't change the past. Bree, if he risked our lives to avoid leaving that model submarine behind in the caves under Loch Ness, when there was not a chance in hell anyone would ever have found it, he wouldn't approve of us trying to stop the *Titanic* from sinking. The Doctor is always telling his companions that he can't interfere with fixed events in time. It causes all sorts of paradoxes and nasty chain events if you do. I'm pretty certain something like the sinking of the *Titanic* would be considered a fixed event in time."

"But these people are all going to die."

"They already have. About a century ago." He paused. "Or in a century's time, depending on how you look at it. Come on, we need to find somewhere private so you can riffle us out of here." Hamish walked off, and Briana had no choice but to follow him, or lose him.

There were people everywhere, so they decided to head back to the cabin they had phphted into. After many mistaken turns they eventually found it, and after Rashid had untoyed Briana explained to him what was going on.

"Mum, you have to riffle us out, you have to get us off here, this ship is gonna go down, it's gonna hit a big cold iceberg and sink into the big cold sea and I can't swim and I don't wanna drown and you have to do something!"

He scrambled up Briana and sat on her shoulder. She took Hamish's hand in her left. "*Riffle out.*" Nothing happened. She clasped her necklace and tried again, a little louder. Still nothing happened. "You try."

Hamish shook his head, "I don't have a necklace."

"No, but you riffled us to Loch Ness."

Hamish tried, but he had no luck either. He held Briana's necklace and tried again, but that still didn't work. In desperation Briana tried once more, shouting "*RIFFLE OUT.*" And still nothing happened.

The *Titanic* had set sail on the last leg of her deadly voyage, and the twins and Rashid were trapped on board.

XVII: The Feadh-Ree

Briana looked at Hamish. "Why isn't it working?"

"How would I know?"

Rashid panicked, "Mum, we're still stuck on this boat and you said it's gonna sink, and I can't swim."

"Hush now, we'll think of something." Briana moved the monkey off her shoulder and rested him on her hip. She looked at Hamish.

"Well, any ideas? We have to get off this boat."

"Ship," he corrected automatically.

"Whatever. Any ideas?"

"Nothing beyond you trying to riffle us out again." He took hold of her hand.

Briana tried, but still nothing happened.

"What does Alasdair do when he riffles out? I mean, does he do anything different from what you do?" Hamish asked.

"I don't think so," Briana replied.

"Bree, what were you thinking of when you tried to

riffle?" A note of excitement had crept into Hamish's voice.

"Getting off this boat before it has a close encounter of the personal kind with an iceberg."

"Were you thinking of where you wanted to riffle us to?"

"Not particularly, I just wanted to get us off the boat."

"Ship." Hamish tried to explain his reasoning. "Look, we know that when you're doing stuff with the Atlas, like dressing yourself, the Atlas dresses you in what you're thinking of, right? So, maybe you need to think of where you want us to go. Maybe thinking 'get us out of here' isn't enough for the Atlas to go on."

"I still have a lot of trouble coming to terms with the idea a book knows what I'm thinking."

Hamish grinned at her. "Well, the ships they found when they first went to Atlantis knew what the pilots were thinking, and the Leviathan ships, the biomechanoids, or living ships, knew what their crew were feeling, so it's not surprising, really, that the Atlas is capable of knowing what you're thinking." He went over and looked out the porthole. "Look, we're nearly out of the harbour. There's a lighthouse, fix that in your mind and try again." He took her hand, while Rashid jumped back to her shoulder.

Briana stared at the little lighthouse, then closed her eyes, and tried to concentrate on its image as hard as she could. "*Riffle out.*"

With relief, she found herself in a tunnel of blue stars before being phphted out onto solid ground next to Hamish and Rashid.

"Okay, we're off the boat, but I still don't believe …" The three of them had not landed anywhere near the lighthouse.

They were, instead, in the middle of a circle of singing and dancing winged creatures. Not only that, but it was no longer day. A full moon now shone on them from the night sky. Briana stood slowly and looked at the members of the circle.

They appeared to be human (apart from the wings), and there seemed to be an even number of males and females. Both genders had long, golden hair that fell almost to the ground on the females, and to the waists of the males. They were all a good two heads taller than the twins.

Their long wings curved up from their shoulder blades and swept down in graceful waterfalls of gleaming white feathers, almost reaching their ankles. They reminded Briana of pictures she had seen of angels' wings in an old children's Bible she had bought at the Lion's Club Book Fair a few years ago because she liked the pictures in it.

The winged creatures were all dressed in robes of silver silk, and had bare feet. The females had gold-painted toenails and wore circlets around their foreheads. Some had simple bands of gold, while others had intricately worked weavings of leaves and berries. It seemed to Briana that most were, perhaps, in their mid-twenties.

Every member of the circle was now staring intently at the two humans and the monkey who had phphted into their midst, although their alabaster faces conveyed no emotion, not even surprise, at the trio's appearance. Rashid had remained untoyed, but he remained untoyed around Alasdair and Glynian. He must only toy around humans, Briana thought.

Rashid leapt into her arms and rained kisses on her face. "You did it Mum, you did it, you saved us, we're off the boat, you saved us from being squashed by an iceberg, or freezing to death, or drowning, you saved us, you rock, Mum!"

Two of the creatures stepped forward, a male and a female. Instead of the circlets worn by the rest of their group, they each wore a crown. Briana guessed they were the leaders.

"Good evening," the male addressed them in a voice that was soft, yet resonated with strength. "I am Cathal Shanahan, the King of the *Feadh-Ree*" (he pronounced it 'Faa Ree'), "and this is my Queen, Cathalrina."

"The *Feadh-Ree*? You mean fairies?" Hamish asked, recognising the name from an on-line gaming adventure he had played last year.

"You humans do sometimes call us fairies, that is true." The tone he used on 'fairies' made his opinion of the term obvious. "The Irish at least grace us with the more formal title of *Sidhe*," (he pronounced it 'Shee'). "However, we do prefer *Feadh-Ree*."

Briana was about to ask where they were, when Rashid wriggled out of her arms. She automatically grabbed at him as he jumped down, and as she did so, her necklace swung out from under her jacket.

There was a sharp intake of breath from the *Feadh-Ree* and many whispers in their strange language. Some of the *Feadh-Ree* pointed at the necklace.

Briana looked at the King. "Do you know about this?" she asked, holding her necklace up. "About the Atlas, I mean?"

"Yes, My Lady Briana, we have known of the Atlas for many centuries, so we know your presence here, and that of Lord Hamish, portends the coming of evil times."

"How did you know our names?" Hamish asked,

exchanging a surprised look with Briana.

"We have known your names since your birth." He paused. "We have difficulty keeping track of human time. How old are you?"

"We're almost sixteen, our birthdays are on March the first."

The King frowned. "Alasdair was supposed to wait until you came of age at twenty-five before giving the Atlas to you. This is almost a decade too early and you are not ready.

"You know Alasdair?" Briana asked in surprise.

"Yes, and it worries me that he has given the Atlas to you so young. You will not come of age until twenty-five and …"

"Twenty-one," Hamish interrupted. "We come of age at twenty-one, not that it really means anything in New Zealand, since the drinking age is eighteen. My friend Christopher says it's an American custom we've adopted as an excuse to have a party."

The King was about to reply when his Queen put her hand on his wrist, and shook her head slightly. The King nodded almost imperceptibly. "This is not good news and we must discuss it some more, but somewhere a little more private would be wise. We will go to the *Sifra*, our city and palace. You will like it there."

He extended a hand toward Briana, while the Queen took Hamish's hand. Briana bent and picked Rashid up again, as the King chanted. "*Morko lye ndu e'a i' talar' a.*"

Briana saw the entire circle of *Feadh-Ree* sink into the grass, taking her, Hamish, and Rashid with them. As the ground closed above her head, she sank into a terrifying blackness.

XVIII: The Sifra

Briana tightened her grip on the King's hand as the ground closed about her, and heard him say, "*Fear not, My Lady, no harm will come to you.*"

The words calmed Briana, although she was confused when she heard the King's voice in her head rather than with her ears. Her confusion gave way to awe as she dropped through the ceiling of an enormous cavern, slowly drifted to the floor, and landed in front of a magnificent silver and pearl palace.

"Fantastic," Hamish exclaimed, as they followed the *Feadh-Ree* along a gold pathway that led to the palace. Hamish skipped ahead and started a conversation with two of the *Feadh-Ree*. Picking Rashid up and trailing along behind Hamish, Briana giggled as the monkey commented, "Hamish is like a little boy in a candy store."

"What's so funny?" Hamish asked, looking back over his shoulder.

"Nothing you'd understand."

Hamish narrowed his eyes at her, and turned back to the *Feadh-Ree* at his side. Briana and Rashid laughed together.

However, Briana did have to admit to herself that the inside of the palace was well worth getting excited about. The beautifully decorated walls were covered with intricate floral paintings, highlighted with inlays of precious stones like emeralds, rubies, sapphires, and amethysts. The floors throughout the palace were of a highly polished dark stone, inlaid with abstract designs in gold and, strangely, paua shell. Thousands of candles in sconces along the walls, carved with images of ivy vines, bathed the palace in a liquid golden light.

The King led them through the winding corridors of the palace, up some stairs, down others, and around corners, until Briana was completely lost. When Rashid became too heavy for her to carry, she put him down, only to find he was scooped up by a *Feadh-Ree*, who moved quickly past her.

As the *Feadh-Ree* turned a corner Briana heard him whisper to Rashid. "We have all missed you so much, especially the children. How has life been treating you in the Antipodes?" Briana stopped right where she was, and a *Feadh-Ree* behind walked straight into her.

He stepped back. "Is something wrong, Lady Briana?"

"Well, no, not wrong exactly, it's just ... have you met Rashid before?"

"Rashid, My Lady?"

"The monkey. Has he been here before? I'm sure I heard a *Feadh-Ree* say everyone had missed him."

"I am sure you are mistaken, My Lady, I do not know this creature." The *Feadh-Ree* continued walking.

Briana stood where she was a moment longer, before

moving once again with the flow of fairies down the corridor. She was sure about what she had heard, but how could that be?

Finally she reached a room that she was told was the Banquet Hall; a large area with an enormous dining table long enough to seat a hundred people on each side.

The hall was filled with *Feadh-Ree* dressed for dinner. Briana stood admiring the variety of gorgeous medieval gowns the females wore in shades of purple, blue, and pink, with elaborate embroidery and beading, and with cords tied around the waist and bust-lines. Unlike the first *Feadh-Ree* they had met, they all wore shoes. Briana guessed the others had taken theirs off when they were dancing.

The males were in shirts of blue, green, or brown, with long sleeves, embroidery on the cuffs, a small collar, and a panel that laced up in the front. They all wore tight black woollen pants and leather boots that came to halfway up their shins, and matched the colour of their shirts.

Looking around for Hamish and Rashid, Briana saw that her brother was now deep in conversation with new *Feadh-Ree*, the ones he was talking to earlier no longer in sight.

Rashid was off in a corner of the room with a group of *Feadh-Ree* children. Narrowing her eyes, Briana watched him. Could she have heard the *Feadh-Ree* correctly? Did these children know Rashid? How was that possible? Shaking her head slightly, she sighed. She might ask Rashid about it later, but for now she felt she'd had enough shocks for one day.

About ten minutes later Briana was considering asking where the fairies they had met above ground were when they reappeared. They had changed into similar clothes to the other *Feadh-Ree*, except that they wore bronze (the females) and silver (the males), whilst the King and Queen were both dressed in gold, the colour matching their crowns.

At the far end of the table two enormous chairs, seemingly made of amethyst, stood side by side. The King assisted his Queen into the right-hand chair, and took the left chair himself. Briana watched as the *Feadh-Ree* Hamish had been talking to indicated to her brother he should sit closest to the King. With a gesture the Queen waved down the table to Briana to join them and take the chair closest to the Queen.

After Briana sat, the rest of the *Feadh-Ree* they had met above ground took the seats closest to the twins, with the females on Briana's side of the table, and the males on Hamish's side. Rashid, somewhat cheekily, scrambled to the top of the King's chair and sat there surveying the room. The remaining *Feadh-Ree* took seats on either side of the table, according to their gender.

The King addressed the twins. "You are fortunate to have dropped in when you did. The Circle was my Council of Advisors, and it is only at the full moon we are all together. For the rest of the time many are away roaming the land."

The sound of a side door opening distracted Briana, and she froze for an instant as Glynian walked through, followed by … many Glynians. But … no, none of them were Glynian. They were, however, all cluricauns. They all looked so alike, and the fact they all wore exactly the same clothes as Glynian didn't make telling them apart any easier. Obviously the race all bore strikingly similar characteristics, and were not sartorially diverse.

The cluricauns carried platters of food, and Briana smiled

when she saw that there was no meat. She misinterpreted Hamish's look of dismay as a silent protest over the vegetarian fare on offer. Briana had no objections, and was about to tuck in when Hamish called her name sharply across the table, and then stopped as if not sure how to continue.

The Queen smiled. "It is a common human belief, is it not, that to eat of fairy food or to drink of fairy wine means the consumer will forget all they have loved in the human world and will remain forever in the land of the fairies?"

A flush coloured Hamish's cheeks, and a chuckle rippled throughout the hall. The Queen continued. "A mythology, Lord Hamish, a legend, which is all those stories are." She paused. "True, sometimes we have kept humans here, possibly against their initial wishes, but it is not our food or drink which has kept them here. We have powers other than that. Please, it is safe for you to eat and drink."

Unconvinced, and not exactly reassured by the Queen's comments, Hamish made no move toward the food. Briana, however, was prepared to take the Queen at her word and lifted a pitcher to fill her glass. The Queen laughed, placing her hand on Briana's wrist.

"Fairy wine, however, is not for human children, nor, for that matter, should it even be consumed by human adults. Some juice for our guests, please," she addressed a cluricaun.

"You all seem to be young, Your Majesty," Briana ventured. "No one here looks to be older than about twenty-five. Are your elders somewhere else?"

"How little you know of our kind, Lady Briana. My husband and I are over five thousand years old."

Briana gaped at the Queen, but before she could say

anything else the King addressed her. "If you would be so kind, My Lady, I would like to hear about everything that has happened to you since Alasdair gave you the Atlas. Since you fell into our Circle I have made a few educated guesses, all of which worry me, and all of which may be wrong. I would like, therefore, to hear your tale, to know whether to stop worrying, or indeed, to know whether I am not worrying nearly enough."

"Cathal, let the poor child eat first, for goodness sake," the Queen chided him.

"That's okay, Your Majesty, I'm not hungry; I'll tell you about it."

Briana knew he was probably starving, Hamish was always hungry, but he was holding back from eating or drinking here, just in case. Briana hesitated, but gave in to her stomach and started to eat, ignoring the slight shake of Hamish's head he directed at her.

Turning to the King, Hamish conveyed everything that had happened to them since that day when Briana first saw Alasdair. As Briana listened it all seemed so long ago, as so much had happened since then, but in actual time it was only a few days since they had arrived in Britain. They had landed in London early Monday morning, and it was now Thursday afternoon, or at least, it was in their own time. Briana wasn't sure what time she was in right now, although she presumed they were still in 1912.

The King looked at the twins after Hamish finished their story.

"So, Alasdair believes that Cadeyrn Llewellyn, the Great Enemy, is to make a move soon to take over the world?"

"The Great Enemy?" Hamish remarked. "I'm guessing that's with a capital 'G' and a capital 'E'. What does that mean, the Great Enemy?"

"You do not know of the Great Enemy? Of the Prophecy?"

Hamish shook his head, but Briana had a vague recollection of the term. "Hamish, remember when we were in that cellar on the far side of Loch Ness, didn't Glynian refer to us as the twin, oh, something to do with a prophecy."

"Oh, yes, that's right, the Twin Heirs of the Prophecy. I'm guessing we get capital letters too, huh? Alasdair wouldn't tell us what was meant by it. Trying to get information out of him is like getting blood out of a stone."

"Do you know what Alasdair meant when he called us 'the Twin Heirs of the Prophecy'?" Briana asked the King.

The King did not immediately reply, and when he did, he did not answer Briana's question. Instead, he asked again, "Does Alasdair believe Llewellyn is soon to make his move?"

"I think so. His theory is Cadeyrn will establish himself as a dictator in his own time, which will flow through to our time, where he'll still be a dictator, but the world won't have all the technology that we currently have, but Cadeyrn will as he will have the discontinued . . . ahh, frequencies, ohh, somethings . . .sorry, that started out so well."

Hamish laughed.

Briana ignored him, and addressed the King again. "Anyway, I'm not sure how it will affect you here in 1912. In the *Sifra*, I mean, not the 1912 up there." She gestured toward the ceiling.

"Is that the year we were in? We do not take much notice

of the human calendar and besides, we move around in human time a lot. What is your current time?"

Briana told him.

Exchanging a glance with the Queen, the King chanted, "*Maer byrn*," causing Briana and Hamish to instantly fall asleep at the table.

"How can they not be aware of who they are?" the King asked his Queen.

"Alasdair must have his reasons for that." She addressed Rashid. "Caranthir, do you, Finrod, or Séreméla have any idea why Alasdair has given the twins the Atlas this early?"

Rashid shook his head, and spoke in a voice different to his usual one. "You know what Hamish said about getting blood out of a stone? So true. That damn gnome has been meticulous in not allowing the three of us to get him alone since he gave the Atlas to Briana." He paused. "Well, Séreméla managed a few words with him after we arrived in Wales, but we didn't know events had escalated at the time, so it wasn't discussed."

The Queen looked at the King. "It would be best if the children do not remember the title the Twin Heirs of the Prophecy until we have had a chance to talk to Alasdair. If they remember it, they will ask too many questions."

"You are right, my dear. *Thysaer Si Sol Caes os si Vydaelia.* Toskinaria," he called to the *Feadh-Ree* who had carried Rashid into the Banquet Hall, "can you and Kaldaria please carry the Twins to the guest room prepared for them? Go with them, Caranthir," he told Rashid. "And be more careful, Toskinaria. Kaldaria reports that the Lady Briana overheard you when you told Caranthir that we've all missed him."

"But you have missed me, haven't you?" Rashid cried cheekily, speaking in his normal voice and jumping into the King's arms.

"That, my dear 'Rashid', is not the point, as you well know. He firmly deposited Rashid on the floor. "Run along now, and try to behave, will you. No wonder you chose a monkey, the form suits your personality so well. And you, Toskinaria, mind your tongue, lad."

"Yes, Your Majesty." Toskinaria looked at the floor with flaming cheeks. He and Kaldaria left the room, carrying a twin each, while Rashid scampered along behind them.

King Cathal looked at Queen Cathalrina. After four thousand years of marriage, they could convey much to each other with one look.

The look the King exchanged with his Queen told her how disturbed he was by the news the twins had brought about Cadeyrn Llewellyn. For the King knew far more about the Great Enemy than the children did. He also knew much more about the Atlas, and he had talked often with Alasdair throughout the centuries. He was keen to talk to the slippery gnome again as soon as possible.

He was particularly concerned about how the children had arrived here in what they thought was the human year 1912. He had not told them, but when they phphted into the *Sidhe* ring they had not come into the human year 1912.

The *Feadh-Ree* had been holding this particular *Sidhe* ring the twins had dropped into in 1172, when war was raging between the Irish, the English, and the Anglo-Normans, and when two strangers in the area would have been killed on suspicion of being spies, regardless of their age.

From what Briana had told him about their movements in time from St. Colman's Cathedral, the King suspected Cadeyrn Llewellyn had sent one of the sentient paradoxical beings known as a Rogue Riffle into the fabric of time to hunt for the Twins. This was what had sent them back to the human year 1912, and then to 1172.

Although Briana believed thinking of the lighthouse had riffled them off the *Titanic*, she was wrong. The Rogue Riffle had obviously found them in St. Colman's Cathedral and it had denied Briana access to her powers.

This Rogue Riffle had initially sent the twins onto the *Titanic* in 1912, but had probably decided too many children survived the disaster so moved them to 1172 instead where it was more likely they would be killed.

Had they not landed exactly where they had, in the middle of the *Sidhe* ring, their chances of surviving would have been slim. The King did not believe in a coincidence of such magnitude, and he suspected Alasdair had played a part in directing the twins to the *Sidhe* ring. Caranthir could not have achieved it in his current form.

For now, the twins were safe. The Rogue Riffle could not enter the *Sifra* to harm them. However, the Rogue Riffle would still be hunting for them, and once it had their scent, it wouldn't stop until it managed to get them killed. If they left the *Sifra*, sooner or later their luck would run out and the Rogue Riffle would send them to a time that would kill them. The twins must not be allowed to leave the *Sifra* again. They were too important to the future of the world for that.

About the author

Karolyn Timarkos has worked as a radio announcer, journalist, graphic designer, website designer, lion and tiger park guide, photographer, and in numerous roles within the hospitality and tourism industries. Her talents include being able to watch an entire season of Doctor Who in one sitting, persisting in a passion for surfing even though after many years she can still only catch white wash, and being able to get around Disney World, Epcot, and Islands of Adventure in one day per park without missing anything.

She loves cats, WOMAD festivals, the Oxford Comma, and travelling. She dislikes smokers, political correctness, and people who don't know the difference between your and you're. Karolyn (or Kaz to her friends) lives in Tauranga, New Zealand, with her Mum and brother (she did leave home for 17 years) and a selection of cats. She misses Ace of Hearts, Jackson, and Oberon every day.

www.karolyntimarkos.com - www.theatlaschronicles.com

I hope you have enjoyed reading Nathar because as I hoped writing it. It would be a huge help to me if you could write a review on Amazon... and one on Goodreads if you are using social whatever. Positive book reviews really help anyone and make my writing.

You can find links to come to post reviews on the website www.thenatharchronicles.com also you never look maybe like photos of the places in the book, movies, and word games. Maybe you can send artwork related to the book and I will post it in the online gallery of fan art.

Warm regards to all

Varolyn Timarkos

Code and pay hi to be in Cyluxylaxy - I hope Hamlig fred by anybody reading

Acknowledgements

It was a very long time from conception to publication, and many, many wonderful people were involved in the process. I wish to make a special thank you to:

Peter E. C. Dashwood for advice on the quantum physics stuff and the first edit of the manuscript way back in 2002.

Holly Bennett, the author of the fantastic *Bonemender* series of books (amongst others), my wonderful and amazing editor, for making my writing oh-so-much better. www.hollybennett.net

Dr. Paul Vincent for the most extraordinary proof reading of the final draft. He even spotted the misspelling of the name of a rap trio from Senegal. www.doctoredit.co.nz

Tami Norman from **Integrity Formatting** for unbelievable service and awesome work. www.facebook.com/IntegrityFormatting

Debbie, Jabba, Christopher, Lachlan, and **Tannesha Jess** for believing in the story for so long.

Hamish and **Ryan Krebs** for sharing your names with a certain young surfer.

Chris and **Sandra Belcham**, the owners and operators of Tyn-y-Bryn Bed & Breakfast in Abergavenny, for allowing me to share your home with Briana and Hamish.

Kristi Clark, for your ongoing support and encouragement, and for handing out all those flyers in King, North Carolina. And to **Chris** and **Donna Clark** for being wonderful.

Mr. Blane William Traynor for your absolute awesomeness, and your amazing Scottishness. Without you, Glynian would have been a horrible, and completely inaccurate, stereotype.

Tim Riley from Dominion Law for legal advice on copyright issues surrounding what fantasy and sci-fi works Hamish, Glynian, and Alasdair could talk about.

Jackie Baldwin, the **Schlecht-Watts**, and **Carrie Jones** for your ongoing support.

Chris Todd, Michelle Todd, Jade Love, Debra Jess, Michelle Clifton, Shae McCracken, Sam Turner, and **Elaine Smit** for helping to rename the book when the title no longer worked.

All the ladies of **Bookrapt** for your years of support and advice, and especially all my friends who are "proper" authors for all their stories of working with traditional big-name publishers. You convinced me that self-publishing is the way of the future.

The Facebook Fans for supporting the first four chapters of an unpublished manuscript. Your kind comments and passion for the story over many years kept me going in the face of all those rejections from traditional publishers.

Jean Bennett for yet another proof-read after I'd mucked around with Holly and Paul's work.

Vincent Porter for the final, final, absolute final, proof-read.

And finally, to the memory of my **Great-Uncle Owen Glyndwr Baker-Gabb** (1924 – 2008) for sharing his love and knowledge of our ancestry with me.

Book two in The Atlas Chronicles® series.

Fifteen-year-old twins Briana and Hamish Ryan continue
their Quest through time, risking their lives to gather
the Elixir Ingredients.

The incredible secret in their thousand-year-old ancestry is
finally revealed to them, which not even Hamish's wildest
sci-fi fantasies could have prepared them for.
But with that truth comes an awful responsibility,
and the thought they may have to make
a terrible choice.

Meanwhile, just as one secret is unravelled, Briana is starting
to wonder about a mystery surrounding Rashid,
even stranger than when the former soft toy came to life.

www.theatlaschronicles.com